PENGUIN VEER

OPERATION PAYBACK

Aditi Mathur Kumar is a proud Indian Army wife. As a civilian married to an army officer, she felt many stories from her life were poignant and the world needed to hear them. Her books are a result of that. Aditi is also the only Indian Army wife to deliver a TEDx talk about the lives of army families.

Her books include *Soldier & Spice: An Army Wife's Life, Love, Whatever That Means* and *This Heartbreak: A Collection of Poems*. Aditi works in advertising and can be found on Twitter and Instagram @adicrazy.

T0096918

Celebrating 35 Years of
Penguin Random House India

OPERATION PAYBACK

ADITI MATHUR KUMAR

PENGUIN
VEER

An imprint of Penguin Random House

PENGUIN VEER

USA | Canada | UK | Ireland | Australia
New Zealand | India | South Africa | China | Singapore

Penguin Veer is part of the Penguin Random House group of companies
whose addresses can be found at global.penguinrandomhouse.com

Published by Penguin Random House India Pvt. Ltd
4th Floor, Capital Tower 1, MG Road,
Gurugram 122 002, Haryana, India

First published in Penguin Veer by Penguin Random House India 2023

ISBN 9780143459880

Typeset in Adobe Caslon Pro by MAP Systems, Bengaluru, India
Printed at Thomson Press India Ltd, New Delhi

www.penguin.co.in

*This is for all the heroes in the Indian Armed Forces
and their brave families.*

*Your heroism inspires me every day, and
I salute each one of you.*

Jai Hind!

1

As the Gypsy moved through the Himalayas, snaking between the three feet of snow that had been recently cut to clear the road, Lieutenant Chauhan, sitting at the back of this fairly camouflaged army vehicle, experienced a sudden rush of emotions. The snow-covered mountains felt strangely familiar, even though the lieutenant had visited this part of the country for the first time only a few days back. The days had been spent scaling mountains laden with thick snow, trying to track signals and interpret messages which were encrypted and dangerous. But the young lieutenant did not mind the hard work.

As the vehicle circled the mountains, going higher and higher to the Indian Army Post, which was their destination, Lt Chauhan stared out at the landscape, almost mesmerized. Clearly, the new officer was still in awe of the haunting beauty of this part of Kashmir; the last few days in this location had not diminished the wonderment that shone in those eyes.

Major Vikram Rana, Sena Medal, the officer sitting in the co-driver seat, turned around and said, 'Kashmir—heaven on Earth. It almost feels like we're in an exotic foreign country, doesn't it?'

'Yes, sir,' replied Lt Chauhan. And then added, 'but it feels familiar at the same time.'

A shadow of sorrow mixed with immense pride crossed Maj. Rana's face.

Lt Chauhan sat there, calm and composed, not betraying the overwhelming emotional rollercoaster this was proving to be.

This is the *karmbhoomi* for heroes, Lt Chauhan thought—something that had kept the young officer motivated over the past few years of turmoil.

2

September 2013

Captain Ranvijay Chauhan, Sena Medal, stood outside his quarters at his Para unit headquarters in Udhampur, J&K, a Borosil glass of steaming tea in his hands. He looked at the crisp, blue sky and wondered what his next call of duty would be, and how soon. Kicking his heels, waiting around at the headquarters wasn't something he enjoyed doing, even when the unit was busy and buzzing.

The mere mention of Capt. Chauhan's formidable Parachute Regiment Special Forces unit was enough to make cross-border infiltrators change their plans, quite literally. And Capt. Chauhan, a counterterrorism specialist, was considered one of the best commandoes because of his expertise on the terrain, his exemplary leadership skills and courage beyond the call of duty. The unit's reputation made it imperative for it to keep its location a secret, and the *paltan*s always kept moving to cover the area for surveillance and operations, hardly ever staying in one place for too long.

Nevertheless, keeping a Para SF unit's presence secret in this area was a tough task. Pakistan's military machinery had an impressive intelligence network along the Line of Control and in J&K. But deception is an art that Para SF was skilled in and like all Para soldiers, Capt. Chauhan was always careful not to give away any hint of their presence. Unlike most army officers, he had a beard and wore civil clothes instead of a uniform. A lot of Para SF commandos in active duty in the area lived like this. Capt. Chauhan also knew the local dialect well and could speak fluently like a native of the area.

He loved the Kashmir valley and was dedicated to his role in restoring peace in the area. To him, it felt like the higher purpose of his life. This is why the young captain had been restless over the past three days, which he and his paltan spent at the headquarters. He knew that his men were just as eager as he was to receive their next assignment, whatever it might be, to break out of this state of limbo.

Only three days ago, his team had put an end to an ongoing encounter between J&K Police and two Lashkar-e-Taiba terrorists in Baramulla. Both the terrorists were eliminated and the Para SF team came out without sustaining any injuries or casualties. This was what mattered most to Capt. Ranvijay Chauhan, and back at the HQ that morning, he felt what he always felt after each of the eight operations he had been involved in till date—a mammoth sense of accomplishment, not only because of the eliminated terrorists, but because, for the eighth time, he was able to return to base with all his men alive and safe.

That was what drove Capt. Ranvijay Chauhan.

When he was commissioned to the Indian Army, he not only vowed to protect his country and his countrymen, he also swore to himself to never take the lives of the exemplary men, his paltan, for granted. Protecting his men on every mission was as crucial to him as the mission itself, and he was proud, almost relieved, every time they returned from a mission, successful and in full strength.

Later that night, Capt. Chauhan sat listening to the radio set in the HQ, indulging in his hobby while he was in between missions and sipping rum. Lance Naik Siddhu, who had been Capt. Chauhan's buddy ever since his induction to the Para SF, and who was one of the most remarkable soldiers the captain knew, was reminiscing about Capt. Chauhan's first mission.

'Vikram Rana sir was supposed to go for the mission, but he and his squad were on a recce at a higher altitude and couldn't trek back in time because of the snow. That was how Chauhan sir was assigned his first mission in the very first month of his joining,' said Siddhu to the radio operator, who was also a trained soldier and part of the same Para unit.

The operator continued with the narrative: 'Saab fired his gun, but the bullet only hit the terrorist's leg. Everyone in the squad assumed that Saab had deliberately shot him in the leg to merely injure the terrorist, but I knew—this was the first time Saab had faced a terrorist . . . his hand had been shaking.'

'I've been with Saab ever since his commissioning, I know him well. I shouted from behind a tree, which was my position, "Saab, next bullet in his head!"

'And then Saab put a bullet into the terrorist's head!' the radio operator triumphantly came to the end of his reminiscence, a tinge of pride in his voice. They were from the same unit after all and the glory was for all of them to share.

'Yes he did!' Lance Naik Siddhu prompted.

'On our way back from the operation, I said to him, "Saab, although they had AK-47s, your own M4A1 5.56-mm carbine got in first and got its first opportunity to fire at the enemy; it's a good beginning."'

'No guts, no glory,' said Capt. Chauhan. 'I learnt the true meaning of this phrase that day, Siddhu.'

It was indeed a good beginning. And Capt. Chauhan's guns did not stop eliminating terrorists ever since that fateful first day. His hands never shook. His aim never wavered. His bullets never missed. And his squad always returned home in full strength.

Time passed and ever since then, this squad took care of many jihadi infiltrations in the Kupwara district—an area that Capt. Chauhan knew like the back of his hand.

* * *

January 2014

The first week of January went by with the squad carrying out desultory patrol duties and while counterinsurgency operations were underway in the area, it had been a few days since Capt. Chauhan had been assigned a mission.

Being highly motivated to stay in action, the entire squad was restless and eagerly looked forward to their next mission. Waiting is not something the Para SF soldiers relished; just as they didn't enjoy time idled away resting in their barracks or being incarcerated at home on leave—they would always rather be on a mission. At dinner at the officers' mess one evening, Capt. Chauhan wondered out loud when they should expect to be briefed for their next op.

And news arrived the very next day.

Two Pakistani terrorists had crossed the LoC and entered the Ramban area. Ramban was situated in the lap of the Pir Panjal range of the mighty Himalayas. The intelligence report said that the two were stealthily making their way across the area, carrying ammunition replenishments that were to be handed over to a Lashkar-e-Taiba group somewhere around Naugam.

Just a week ago, their formation had been informed by Indian intelligence that they had picked up tips about a brutal assault being planned in a crowded public place in Srinagar by the extremely radical terror group, Lashkar-e-Taiba. The intel was not specific at the time, and not corroborated. But now, the new report of this infiltration indicated that this public attack was indeed a possibility, and the ammunition was being supplied from across the border.

With this quick development, the Corps had to take quick action to maintain peace in the region, and Capt. Chauhan's Para SF unit was assigned to the task.

Their orders were simple: intercept the two terrorists in the Ramban area, so that the exchange of arms doesn't happen, and the plan could thus be nipped in the bud.

Intercepting the terrorists meant only one thing for Para SF—this was not a unit that was deployed for defence: the job of the Para SF was to attack and to terminate. Capt. Chauhan was ready for his ninth mission.

He would lead the operation with his team of six Para SF soldiers, and they would try to 'make contact'—Para SF language for 'attack'—in the tough and hilly terrain of Ramban, stopping them before they entered Naugam.

The terrain was a hostile one, but it provided the means to make a good escape, which was why terrorists always selected such areas. This terrorist duo had almost been waylaid by a paltan of Rashtriya Rifles two nights ago, but they had managed a clever escape, taking advantage of the Himalayan landscape and their terrorist training in evasion.

Immediately afterwards, Rashtriya Rifles relayed the information to intelligence units in the area, and the terrorists were tracked using a Searcher Mark II drone. The issue, however, was that the drone's thermal sensing was picking up very low signals because of the thick tree cover and caves in the area. Also, the two terrorists were keeping their movements minimal during the day; they were smart enough to maintain a low profile and avoid being detected by the drone's surveillance equipment.

This is when the Para SF was called in, because the army didn't want to waste any more time.

Immediately after the briefing, Capt. Chauhan and six of the toughest soldiers of this Para SF unit were lifted off from Udhampur by an army Dhruv chopper. Upon landing, Capt. Chauhan called for a quick group huddle to go over the execution plan for the operation. It was simple: the fully armed group would head to the terrorists' suspected bolthole, cordon off the area and then scan it, inch by inch.

Each man was carrying a combat weight of over 40 kg, and the trek from landing to the suspected area of the terrorists' hideout was all uphill.

The men made their way to the location quickly and quietly, maintaining their camouflage. It was still daylight and they needed to stay hidden until they made their first contact with the terrorists. In about fifty-five minutes, they were close. Capt. Chauhan was leading the group, and suddenly, at a spot behind a thick tree trunk, he motioned for the troop to stop and stay quiet. He had noticed something.

Directly in his line of sight, Capt. Chauhan could see a man sitting with his back against a boulder, amidst the thick green foliage. He had a weapon that looked like an AK-47 on a sling and was focused on something in his hands, something small. *Could be a pistol or grenade*, Capt. Chauhan thought as he spied on the man. Given the location and the weapons, it was clear that this was one of the two terrorists. The Para SF team had to tread carefully. The terrorist was wearing a combat-print jacket, which was one of Capt. Chauhan's pet peeves. You must earn your right to wear combat, he believed, and it should be by swearing on your life to protect innocent lives. Every time he encountered a terror-motivated, brainwashed, armed man in combat, Capt. Chauhan's blood boiled.

Capt. Chauhan decided to wait for a few long minutes and observe, because it was clear that the terrorists were oblivious to the Para SF's presence at their lair. It was a good opportunity to scan the area and possibly locate the second terrorist as well, in order to minimize any unpleasant surprises for his squad. He gestured to his men to take positions and stay down.

After about fifteen careful minutes, the other terrorist walked into sight. He was wearing a full-length, brown *pheran*, and he didn't seem to be carrying any weapon that was big enough to be put on a sling behind his back or tucked under his arm. That ruled out any LMG or assault rifles, Capt. Chauhan assessed, nonetheless he could still be carrying small arms or grenades and Capt. Chauhan wanted to be careful. As the second terrorist went up and sat against a boulder diagonally opposite to the first one, Capt. Chauhan noticed something suspicious.

Did he just nod in the direction opposite to the first terrorist?

It definitely seemed like he had. The area the terrorist had indicated was, at that moment, not within Capt. Chauhan's range of sight. The intel was on two terrorists, but there might be a surprise here, he thought to himself. This changed things.

Siddhu, who was right behind Capt. Chauhan, crept closer and whispered in trained sotto voce, 'Saab, *aage badhey?*'

'There is someone else. A third person,' Capt. Chauhan replied, his eyes fixed in the direction of the hideout. He could still see both terrorists. They weren't talking at all and seemed to be eating a snack of some sort which they were carrying in small drawstring bags.

'Saab, we have intelligence information for two.'

'We can't take the risk. Let's wait and watch.'

'Saab, together, this squad has taken on many terrorists in the past. We can easily handle three.'

Capt. Chauhan was not convinced. He knew he'd seen the almost indistinct nod, and he couldn't ignore it. 'We can't say anything for sure, Siddhu. If there are more, this could be a suicide mission.'

'They are just two there, saab; the intelligence was solid. And no one could've joined them in Ramban because Rashtriya Rifles has closed off the area and the BSF squad is also out on patrol.'

Capt. Chauhan looked behind him at the formation. The group was alert and eager to finish this mission as soon as they could. After all, how much of a fight could two weather-worn terrorists offer to these tough Para SF soldiers? In fact, this was the reason why only six—a number Siddhu thought was two men too many to tackle two terrorists—had been assigned to this task.

They had waited for almost half an hour now. There was no sign of anyone else besides the two terrorists who were in line of sight. It was obvious that they were waiting for nightfall to set off on their journey. *Did I imagine that barely perceptible nod?* Capt. Chauhan wondered, looking up at the sky.

Night would fall in an hour or so; he had to move fast. He shook his head and shook away his doubt with it and signalled the squad to attack. The six men took up position in a semicircle and closed in towards the target, weapons at the ready and aimed. Capt. Chauhan had the straight route and he led the group from the front.

Siddhu, who was directly behind Capt. Chauhan, followed closely.

The tactic would have been very simple—considering the location of both the terrorists was already known, the squad would take them by surprise by opening fire from close range. But as per standard procedure, for all operations taking place on Indian territory, the army could not directly shoot or take any hostile action unless challenged and confirmed.

The two men were clearly jihadis, but Capt. Chauhan knew he had to challenge the two—there was no way around protocol. But he also knew that challenging the terrorists only handed them an upper hand over the defence forces because it instantly gave away the squad's position, robbing them of the element of surprise and offering the terrorists the opportunity to attack first. Gesturing to his squad to stay agile, he aimed his gun at the one he had spotted first, and spoke from behind the tree.

'*Kaun ho tum log? Apni pehchaan batao!*'

At this, both men grabbed their weapons, the first one, his rifle, and the second one—Capt. Chauhan had been right—took out a pistol from his waistband, getting ready to fire. But the Para SF squad was prepared for this; it was not their first encounter led by a challenge, obviously.

In a split second, and before the two terrorists could fire their weapons, both were taken down. Capt. Chauhan took on the first terrorist, who was getting in position to fire. The bullet lodged itself firmly in his forehead before he could press the trigger. Capt. Chauhan realized that the thing in his hand was a tiny phone, which dropped to the side as the bullet hit him. The second terrorist was killed immediately and simultaneously by the squad, and he collapsed on the spot.

Suddenly, a fresh fusillade of bullets flew towards them from another direction.

There *is* someone else here, Capt. Chauhan thought, just as Siddhu jerked his head towards him, as if thinking the same thing. Ordering the squad to take cover and fire, Capt. Chauhan moved behind a boulder to assess the situation.

The gunfire was erupting from just one source, he determined. And this wasn't someone with skilled aim either, that much was clear. Whoever was firing this fresh volley was either nervous as hell or untrained—the latter seemed unlikely to Capt. Chauhan, based on his past encounter operations. Most terrorists who were dispatched to carry out specific tasks from across the border were skilled at their weapons. The captain was sure that the poor aiming was probably due to a case of nerves upon coming face-to-face with death at the hands of the Indian Army.

The direction from which the gunfire was coming was thick with undergrowth and trees; so visibility was low when compared to the thin cover of foliage for the squad right now and in this juxtaposition of the evening light, the Para SF paltan was exposed. There was only one way to tackle this, thought Capt. Chauhan.

And so, he did. He told Siddhu to provide him with covering fire and scurried over to the next tree and then on to the next, three soldiers following him as he did so. This was a manoeuvre the squad had practised several times, but it was their first live-action test.

A few trees ahead, Capt. Chauhan spotted not one, but two, terrorists crouched behind a boulder, both wearing combat jackets. One of them was randomly firing from an AK-56 in all directions, a sure sign of an untrained soldier, maybe a rookie who wasn't expected to fight this gunfight.

The other one, Capt. Chauhan noticed, was cowering against the boulder, gripping his knees to his chest and seemingly speaking, or reciting, something in panic, his hands to his ears. He couldn't have been much older than sixteen or seventeen, Capt. Chauhan thought, as he crept towards the gunman. Capt. Chauhan took a direct shot at him, instantaneously killing him. At the same time, the fourth one was taken down by several bullets from the soldiers beside Capt. Chauhan, and he fell to his side, lifeless.

Both looked younger than your typical terrorists, Capt. Chauhan noticed, and winced at the way such young boys, lads of school-going age, were recruited on these desperate terror missions.

Capt. Chauhan noticed some sacks and wooden crates lying around.

The squad was still on high alert, ready to act if there were other hostile forces hiding in the trees. Suddenly, the familiar tune of a popular phone brand broke the silence. Treading carefully, Capt. Chauhan motioned to the soldiers to stay in position as he moved towards the sound. And he found it.

Beside the fourth and the youngest terrorist who now lay dead was a mobile phone, which explained why he had looked like he was talking animatedly. He had been on a call with someone, thought Capt. Chauhan, and realized this could be a sign of more terrorists incoming. Picking up the device, Capt. Chauhan gave orders for a thorough recce of the area. The phone stopped ringing.

Capt. Chauhan looked around. Counterterrorism operations in this valley never proceeded as expected, but this was a serious lag in definitive information. Had the squad of his six brave soldiers not acted swiftly and shot accurately, this operation could have gone sideways. With four terrorists who were as ready to sacrifice their lives as they were to take other lives, his team of six could have proved to be too lean.

Capt. Chauhan knelt to examine one of the packages and found four AK-56s with enough ammunition to run several rounds on each. It would be taken back to the headquarters, along with the crates and the sacks.

Although Capt. Chauhan was just a young captain in the Indian Army, his field of expertise was counterterrorism operations, and his experience in this area had taught him a lot. He understood that the presence of two undetected terrorists with this huge dump of weapons meant that a big attack had been in the works, which his squad had probably, hopefully, just foiled.

Although it had ended well, he was still not happy about having gone against his better judgement of not waiting to determine the exact number of terrorists. Capt. Chauhan shook his head as he walked back and picked up the mobile phone that was lying beside the first terrorist. These were crucial to gather more intelligence and, in some cases, produce as evidence by the government on the international level.

I should've waited, he thought. In any case, Capt. Chauhan felt an overall sense of relief that none of his men were hurt. *Despite the massive risk and inaccurate intelligence, this had been easy*, he thought. *What if the other two had been trained terrorists like the first two? Who were the two who had slipped in undetected by intelligence? Is Pakistan now sending children across the border to kill innocent people? Why didn't the fourth one have any weapons on him?* Capt. Chauhan's mind was abuzz with the unanswered questions as he moved around the area to take stock. Just then, the phone which he had picked up from the fourth terrorist started to ring again. The recce was completed by now and the area was clear, so this time, Capt. Chauhan answered the call.

3

The Para SF soldiers looked tensely at Capt. Chauhan as he held the phone to his ear.

'*Sab khair*? Junaid (all well)? a male voice enquired from the other end.

'*Kaun*?' Capt. Chauhan said.

The voice on the other side fell silent.

'I asked, who this is,' repeated Capt. Chauhan.

Silence.

'We have killed four people—which one of them was Junaid?' Capt. Chauhan said, hoping to get a response.

'*Ya* Allah!' The voice quavered this time. It was almost as if the man at the other end of the line had wailed in physical pain like a wounded animal. 'Ya Allah!'

'All four have gone to Allah. Now it's your turn,' said Capt. Chauhan, grimly.

After several seconds of silence, the man at the other end spoke again; this time, in a chilling voice: 'You will pay for this.'

And then, the line went dead.

Back at the headquarters, the squad handed over the captured stock of arms, ammunition and other items to the authorities, including the mobile phones. A special Indian Army unit had been summoned to the spot to secure the area and take the bodies in possession for identification.

After the debriefing later that night, Capt. Chauhan received a visitor in his quarters. Capt. Vikram Rana, a fellow officer, Capt. Chauhan's senior by only a course, came to meet his good friend and to congratulate him on yet another successful operation.

'Meera has called me six times already. My buddy thinks I've got a new girlfriend! Please call her and get me off the hook,' Capt. Rana joked.

'I did, I did!' Capt. Chauhan laughed. He knew just how persistent his wife could be. Capt. Chauhan had got married a couple of years ago; his wife, Meera, was currently in Pune working for the IT giant, Infosys. She was also waiting for him to get a peace posting so they could be together again.

Oh Meera, Capt. Chauhan thought with a smile; *she's relentless*. She knew that Capt. Chauhan couldn't share his whereabouts or missions with anyone; this was just part of the army wife role. Nevertheless, she insisted on knowing that he was okay and listening to his voice at the end of each day—just as any woman in love would. And Capt. Chauhan understood this. Perhaps, in retrospect, sharing Capt. Rana's number with her had not been such a good idea, he thought and chuckled to himself.

'Oh, thank the lord! She might have called our old man next, demanding a report,' Capt. Rana joked.

Officers often referred to their commanding officer as their 'old man'. Capt. Chauhan knew this was a dangerous possibility. When Meera set her mind to something, nothing could stand in her way. His fierce wife followed no rules and let nothing stop her until she got what she wanted.

Smiling, he genially invited Capt. Rana over for a drink. The friends and brother officers had rum and Coke as they caught up, discussing the operations in which they had been involved recently, exchanging notes and joking plenty.

The next day, Capt. Chauhan was summoned by the unit's commanding officer.

'You will move to a different location, Chauhan,' said the CO. 'At least until the dust settles on this one.'

'What dust, sir?' Capt. Chauhan asked, mystified. The CO just looked enigmatically at him. 'Sir, is there something I should know?'

'Ranvijay, nothing is confirmed yet, but the young chap in Ramban is suspected to have been related to a high-profile Lashkar-e-Taiba member; and the contact you had with him on the mobile device puts you in danger of being recognized and targeted.'

Whether the Indian government liked it or not, the militancy intelligence network was deep-rooted in troubled areas like Kashmir, and established terror organizations like Lashkar were known to plant their own spies in India with the sole aim of gathering intelligence about the movements of the Indian Army, especially its special postings and strategic plans.

In the aftermath of certain high-impact operations, the Indian government has been known to provide undercover protection to soldiers involved in operations because of threats made publicly or due to the likelihood of the enemy seeking revenge to make a statement.

'Who?' Capt. Chauhan asked calmly.

'Who what?'

'Who is this high-profile, Lashkar-e-Taiba member whom you just mentioned, sir?'

'Nothing is confirmed yet, Ranvijay,' the CO warned. 'The move, it's to keep your identity safe.'

'Sir, please tell me what you know. I've returned from nine operations now, and this is the first time I'm being asked to run to safety. I think you'll agree with me when I say that I deserve to know whose cage I seem to have rattled.'

The CO looked at the younger officer's calm face. He had been Capt. Chauhan's brother officer ever since the day he had been commissioned to this Para SF unit. The CO had been second-in-command then, and he was particularly fond of Ranvijay. The young chap was right, the CO thought, he deserved to know. If anything, Capt. Chauhan had earned the right to know.

'Sir?' Capt. Chauhan prompted, breaking the CO's reverie.

'Khayyam,' said the CO finally and wondered whether hearing this name would disconcert Capt. Chauhan; but just as he had expected, the captain's expression remained deadpan.

'Khayyam,' Capt. Chauhan repeated.

'Yes.'

'He is hardly some "high-profile" Lashkar-e-Taiba member,' Capt. Ranvijay Chauhan sounded amused. 'He has been the bloody chief of Lashkar-e-Taiba for the last nineteen months.'

Such exceptional mettle, grit and courage in the face of ever-present danger was what Capt. Chauhan and all Para SF soldiers were made of. Not a trace of fear, only a zealous sense of duty and lionhearted bravery.

'The current chief of Lashkar-e-Taiba. Yes,' agreed the CO. 'The fourth chap your team gunned down was apparently Khayyam's youngest brother.'

'He *was* young.'

'Sixteen. Reportedly training for combat in the Lashkar-e-Taiba terror camp in POK for the last month or so,' the CO shared.

'So, he wasn't even properly trained. What was he doing here, on our side of the land with all the others and all that weaponry?' Capt. Chauhan wondered aloud.

'According to what we know—and we don't know a lot—he was here to experience the LOC for the first time along with another trainee. Looks like their job was to hand over a shipment of ammunition to another group of Lashkar terrorists and return to base. But apparently, they decided to accompany the other two and entered India. It is unclear what prompted the two terrorist trainees to stray from their assigned mission, but indications are that they were nearly intercepted by a Rashtriya Rifles *tukdi* on patrol and while escaping, the two older terrorists took them under their wing.'

'He was training to be a terrorist to harm Indian people. If they can train at sixteen, we will have to eliminate at sixteen,' Capt. Chauhan said.

'God knows how many innocents these sixteen-and seventeen-year-olds might have killed if we hadn't intercepted them,' the CO agreed, nodding. And then continued after a pause, 'Listen to me, Ranvijay, we can't risk identification. Go to Jammu for a month or so and we'll have you back here in a jiffy. We can't keep you away from where the action is, so you'll be back soon.'

Capt. Chauhan knew that resisting would be futile; such decisions came from way above the CO's level, and he knew they were right. Khayyam was the fiercest Lashkar-e-Taiba chief in the last decade. More than being a religiously or monetarily motivated terrorist, he was a strategist. And a vicious one. Capt. Chauhan remembered the sound of his voice. While he wanted to stay in action, he knew there was no way he could fight this directive. He nodded and saluted the CO.

For the next two months, Capt. Ranvijay Chauhan spent his days in an office room as an attachment to the Infantry Div. in Jammu, and a delighted Meera—whose company had allowed her to work remotely—joined him for the duration.

4

Meera was not happy.

She had packed a big bag of her things when she left Pune almost two months ago, and had sat through the seemingly endless train journey to Jammu, determined to make the most of this time with her husband. And today, she was going to catch the same train back to Pune, back to her job. Even though she loved her job—she was working with Infosys and had just shifted from their Mysore campus to the one in Pune, which had been part of her career plan for a long time—she did not like the current situation. She found it unbearably sad that, after more than a couple of years of marriage, she still felt like she never had enough time with Ranvijay. She did not want to be away from him.

It was true, they had been married for approximately two years now, but Ranvijay was an army officer—a Para commando, at that!—and while he loved Meera immensely, his duty for the nation outweighed all else, and Meera understood this at most times. Meera knew that a soldier's first love would always be his country; duty would always trump love. But this knowledge wasn't easy. Knowing something in your head was very different from feeling it in your heart. Meera knew Ranvijay had a bigger responsibility, a noble cause even, to protect his nation, but she still felt bad about the long and frequent separations.

People often told her that army wives are supposed to be strong, but she vehemently denied this universal view; it seemed naïve to her. Why do army wives have to be strong? she'd protest passionately. We did not undergo a long training; we were not taught to be an army wife by experts; and we haven't had any prior experience of carrying out the massive onus of an army wife through carefully planned exercise camps, war games or tactical courses.

Army wives learn on the go; they learn though their own experiences of loneliness, through the longing for a normal life and through the ever-present fear of 'what if', which is part and parcel of being an army wife. There's a popular saying about army wives: 'She who waits, also serves', and Meera believed that to serve properly, army wives needed more support and counselling, instead of the almost dictatorial take on mandatory strength for army wives, that is expected to be grasped magically, almost overnight.

'And no, we didn't sign up for it—the separation, the anxiety,' she'd add, concluding her argument.

People who made the well-meaning mistake of imparting anachronistic *gyan* to Meera would often leave with their tails between their legs because Meera was nothing if not impulsive and opinionated. And while she often got into trouble for her headstrong attitude with both their parents, who came from very orthodox Rajasthani Rajput backgrounds, Ranvijay loved Meera's spirit. They were a good match, each a perfect fit to the other's complicated temperament, much like a jigsaw puzzle. Meera resented being made to stay away from Ranvijay.

Meera had been busy studying in Bikaner after the wedding—she had been doing her engineering when she got married—with strong support from Ranvijay, despite her father-in-law's and own dad's vehement opposition to her determined academic pursuit. And in June 2013, she was selected by Infosys during a college placement drive and had moved to Infosys Mysore for training, before being transferred to Pune. Meera hailed from a conservative background in which girls were not expected to be career-oriented. Ranvijay supporting her ambitions meant a lot to Meera. She missed him when he was posted in remote locations and often asked when he would get a peace posting so they could live together, at least for a couple of years.

As a Para commando, Ranvijay's peace posting was almost a myth. He was required at the battlefront—a position he thrived in, but he understood Meera's sentiments and was glad they had enjoyed at least these two months of togetherness.

Now, it was time to part: Ranvijay had been summoned back to his unit, and Meera would reluctantly return to Pune.

'I don't know how to live without you,' she said tearfully to Ranvijay at the railway station. 'I don't know why I have to.'

'Meera, I'll be back for a whole month in April.'

'I don't want a month. I want forever,' Meera pouted.

'We have forever.'

'Do we?'

'We do,' Ranvijay said confidently, kissing her forehead tenderly. 'Until April, then. Know that it is your love that motivates me to carry out my duty to the best of my capabilities.'

'I'm pretty sure the beautiful valley motivates you more than my love.'

'That too!' Ranvijay laughed. 'And as always, I will give you a detailed description of that beautiful place we call India's heaven.'

'Promise?'

'Promise.'

'Well, take care of yourself until then. Don't go crazy chasing after the terrorists trying to become a hero or whatever.'

'No one "becomes" a hero, remember? You either are or you aren't.' Ranvijay said with a smile on his face. 'But point noted, ma'am. Won't go crazy chasing terrorists.'

Meera smiled back. The complicated concept of heroism wasn't what she wanted to discuss at such a moment. She hugged Ranvijay tightly before getting on the train.

* * *

Back again at his Para SF headquarters in J&K, Capt. Chauhan felt immediately ready for the next challenge. The intelligence units had confirmed there was no looming threat of vengeance by the Lashkar-e-Taiba baying for his blood. Nothing ominous had cropped up on the intercepted radio channels and absolutely nothing through the on-ground network either.

His elongated period of absence from the scene of action, where things moved too fast and too unpredictably, served Capt. Chauhan well. He had grown out his beard, as many Para SF commandoes in action areas tend to do and planned to add a few more para jumps to his record—something all Para SF officers enjoyed doing. He also got a chance to study his tactical strategy on ground from various angles. He was aware that his recent success in the Ramban operation was much discussed in the media, even though intelligence agencies were able to contain sensitive details. All that the media knew and talked about for almost four days on prime-time debates and self-congratulatory 'News Specials' was that a courageous team of patriotic 'desh bhakt' Para SF commandoes foiled a potentially devastating terrorist threat in Kashmir by dispatching four terrorists to their seventy-two virgins in a direct encounter.

While they were in Jammu, he and Meera had watched the special coverage and news features and chuckled at the way the media sensationalized things without knowing any of the details that actually mattered. Sometimes he wondered what would happen if the news leaked out that Khayyam Anwar's youngest brother, whom Khayyam loved like he were his own son, had been gunned down in this operation. It would cause a media frenzy, with hour-long heated debates, where everyone from decorated veterans to political science students would opine. News channels would also make it out to be a political assassination, even though the country's politics rarely had anything to do with terror ops by the Forces, at least not directly. Capt. Chauhan was convinced that it was a good thing that this crucial bit hadn't been disclosed to the paparazzi.

Meera had bombarded her husband with a volley of questions to figure out exactly how much of the media's narrative was fact and how much, fiction. Although Capt. Chauhan was not at liberty to share every detail with Meera, he told her what he could. When he described the incident to her, with as much detail as he was allowed to reveal, her beautiful eyes welled up, especially when he mentioned the grim voice on the phone that day, threatening him. Naturally, he didn't tell her who that had been.

Although she claimed that the sinister phone conversation was the part that gave her the shivers, Meera knew there must be something bigger at play this time; something so serious that Ranvijay had to be sent away. She didn't buy into the deputation-for-a-few-months story which Ranvijay fed her but, as an army wife, she knew not to push for information which was most probably classified and she wasn't cleared to know it. Nevertheless, she knew something huge had gone down and that was why every time Ranvijay talked about the threat on that phone call, she got the heebie-jeebies.

Ranvijay understood her foreboding. The whole incident was far from normal, even for a Para SF officer. That was why, he often told her and himself, his time away from the valley had been a necessity.

Now his vacation time was over, and he was back where the action was—ready to do his duty, foil some more terrorists' plans and keen to rejoin his paltan and his soldiers.

He waited eagerly for the next set of instructions and knew it would not be long in coming. Although the valley was beautiful, it wasn't idyllic; anti-Indian forces didn't take breaks and every week there was new intelligence on terror activities. In Kashmir, the Para SF was always on standby, alert and ready for action—as were the BSF, the J&K Police and the other arms of the Indian Army.

For a few long weeks, Capt. Chauhan patrolled the area around Kupwara with his team—their new location. He was forbidden from getting in touch with his on-ground information network—something he was very good at and had taken pains to cultivate. The intelligence might have cleared him of any imminent threat, but they still wanted to keep his identity safe and the informant network in J&K was fairly volatile.

Capt. Chauhan's next operation came to him just as he and his tukdi were halfway through patrolling a sensitive area. They were recalled and asked to report to the CO immediately.

Within two hours, they were back at the unit and were briefed about their next task. The tip-off was about two jihadi recruits spotted on the outskirts of Tangdhar, who were currently hiding in the thick forest on the mountainside. This was the time of the year when young rookies were deployed to the Indian side of the fence to carry out low-scale terrorism activities and prove their mettle, to prepare them for bigger attacks. This was the case with the two jihadis who were currently hiding out in the woods near Tangdhar as per the radio messages caught and deciphered by Indian intelligence and then reported to Para SF. The terrorists had to be stopped at any cost to avoid civil damage.

Capt. Chauhan and his team were dropped close to the location by Dhruv helicopters the same night, and they immediately began their trek upwards, with visibility that was never further than four metres through the thick undergrowth.

The squad of six soldiers, including and led by Capt. Chauhan, knew this was a simple enough task. Newbies were often easy to capture or eliminate given their lack of experience in the terrain. When they were just about to reach the specified location, Capt. Chauhan ordered the squad to split into two groups, and they carefully made their way up, towards the suspected bolthole. While army intelligence had provided a tentative location, there was no way of knowing whether the terrorists had moved since last spotted. So, Capt. Chauhan and team were alert, agile and ready for last-minute surprises. The group moved stealthily through the thick forest, letting their eyes grow accustomed to the gloom of the lush foliage.

Approximately a kilometre-and-a-half ahead of the location specified by the intelligence information, Lance Naik Siddhu detected movement nearby, and upon receiving the signal from him, the group stopped to observe. The intelligence tip was solid, Capt. Chauhan thought, because he spotted two figures dressed in heavy combat jackets, seated on a fallen log in the middle of a cluster of tall trees.

But first, as always, the Para SF commandoes were supposed to challenge the infiltrators.

Signalling his team to stay in position, ready to fire, Capt. Chauhan called out from the shadows, demanding to know who the two individuals were. Pat came the answer. AK-47s started firing on the Para SF commandoes instantly.

As close fire exchange continued, Capt. Chauhan noticed that one of the jihadis had taken a hit in his arm, and was retreating diagonally, looking over his shoulder as if for support. Capt. Chauhan was taken aback by this extremely subtle, almost too-easy-to-miss movement because, in his experience, an injured enemy tends to take cover or tries to escape taking advantage of the terrain. Something wasn't quite adding up, so he shouted out over the gunfire to alert his troop.

Just as he had anticipated, within seconds, a loud explosion shook the forest of Kupwara. An under-barrel grenade-launcher had been fired at the squad, and shrapnel from the exploding grenade injured three of his soldiers. Capt. Chauhan saw them bleeding and he knew this was not the simple task they had anticipated. These were not rookies; there were more than two terrorists; and they were in possession of advanced weapons.

For all Indian Army soldiers, the only impulse stronger than eliminating the enemy, is the duty to help an injured comrade. Capt. Chauhan commanded Lance Naik Siddhu to take the injured commandoes, one by one, to the edge of the forest from where they had entered the woods—a place which was at a lower altitude—and radio for support.

'Rescuing our injured squad members is our topmost priority right now, Siddhu,' Capt. Chauhan told his buddy. 'We'll get these bastards next time.'

Siddhu nodded and leaped into action. He knew his saab was right; the injured commandoes needed to be saved. Amidst gunfire that was now coming in from both sides, Siddhu grabbed one of the three injured commandoes, Naik Kishore bhai. Stealthily and carefully, he carried him out, trekking back on the same route they had followed to get here. As soon as they were about a kilometre from the scene of engagement, Siddhu radioed HQ for help, conveyed their coordinates and then hurried back to the combat zone. Help was on its way, but he had to rescue two more of his buddies. Meanwhile, his saab, along with the other and only remaining commando, Naik Manoj Kumar, held the fort. For the first time since he had been Capt. Chauhan's buddy in combat and in the squad which had successfully carried out nine operations, Siddhu felt that six commandoes were not enough for a mission.

Meanwhile, Capt. Chauhan ordered Naik Manoj Kumar to give him cover fire by staying behind him as he edged towards the two injured soldiers who were yet to be rescued. He wanted to check on them and ascertain that their injuries were not fatal. The gunfire continued unabated from both sides as Capt. Chauhan took cover amidst the trees, and with the help of Naik Manoj Kumar's cover fire, he inched forward. When he was about twenty-five metres away from where he thought his two injured commandoes were, he heard Naik Manoj Kumar groan aloud.

Naik Manoj Kumar had caught a bullet. Capt. Chauhan stopped and dropped to the ground to take cover, anxiously waiting for a signal from Manoj to know that he was okay. A few seconds later, Naik Manoj signalled that he was fine; the bullet had only grazed the flesh on his arm as it had flown past. His groan had been more out of disappointment than pain—he didn't want anything to hinder him from completing this mission with his troop leader. Taking cover behind a tree, he quickly fashioned a cloth bandage and deftly wrapped it around his arm to staunch the bleeding. The squad always came prepared for such incidents. It was bleeding, but it was only a flesh wound which could be dealt with later, he decided. He assured Capt. Chauhan via gestures and signals that he was good to go.

The other side was still firing heavily, targeting the area where Manoj was. His grunt of pain must have given away his position. Using quick gestures, Capt. Chauhan ordered him to not fire any more, to stay low and move away in a circle from his spot, so that the enemy couldn't locate him.

As Naik Manoj Kumar began retreating from his position as per orders, Capt. Chauhan refocused on his objective and crept ahead. So as to not give away his position to the terrorists, Capt. Chauhan did not return the fire which was blazing down from the other side. Within a minute, he had neared the spot where the injured soldiers lay and took cover behind a massive moss-covered tree. Still in a crouched position, Capt. Chauhan decided to edge forwards to assess the situation before beginning their rescue. However, before he could sneak a quick look from behind the tree, the barrage of gunfire from the other side stopped abruptly. This was unexpected in an ongoing skirmish. Capt. Chauhan immediately flattened himself down in the same position, to take stock of the surroundings.

About one hundred metres away, camouflaged by the luxuriant foliage, Naik Manoj Kumar was keeping low and crawling sideways from his spot as instructed by

Capt. Chauhan. The aim was to get as far away as possible from his original position from where he had been firing and had been hit, to make it difficult for the enemy to target him again. *Perhaps my involuntary yelp when the bullet struck me has made the gunmen assume I'm down for good,* Naik Manoj Kumar thought. *This can be to our advantage,* he decided, and started to move quickly to find a vantage point.

However, as Naik Manoj Kumar crept away, the area's low visibility had been worsening by the minute and he couldn't see beyond four or five metres. This is why when he eventually peeked out from behind a tree, he didn't see what Capt. Chauhan saw.

5

Lying prostate in the thick grass of the forest's floor, on his elbows, gun in hand and peering out warily from behind the tree, Capt. Chauhan saw that his commandoes were not only injured by the shrapnel, they were also tied up and gagged. More than fifteen jihadis, holding heavy weapons, surrounded them, but all eyes were on him, as if they had known his position all along and had deliberately chosen to not fire at him; waiting for this moment almost gleefully.

In that moment, Capt. Chauhan realized that this was not about some rookies infiltrating the border as a test. This was a setup.

The only sound he could hear was the whistling of the cold wind, faintly rustling the treetops high above them.

He looked around him, at the strange tableau. The unexpected group of heavily armed terrorists looked like they were ready for war, their guns trained on him; and yet they seemed to be in no hurry to attack him. He allowed himself a quick glance at his wounded squad mates, on their knees, bleeding and gagged. He instinctively knew that this wasn't about them—it was about him. Every glinting eye glaring at him told him that this elaborate trap had been designed solely for his benefit. How? he could not explain, but he knew it in his gut. And yet, the only thing he wanted in that moment was to be able to rescue his men.

Surrounded by the bristling guns of the terrorists who were holding his wounded squad members hostage, Capt. Chauhan stood up and did the only thing he could in the moment—he was sure there was no way that he and his commandoes could get out of this predicament unscathed. He wasn't really worried about himself, but he did want to do everything in his power to save his injured mates.

He stood up from his crouch and demanded in a strong voice, 'What is this cowardice? There's no glory in taking down an injured soldier. Let them go because I'm here for an equal combat.'

'I'm not here for them. They're of no use to me,' a voice boomed from somewhere beyond his line of vision. Capt. Chauhan narrowed his eyes in that direction. A figure, tall and lithe, strolled leisurely out of the shadows. Clad in combat-print baggy pants and a dark jacket, the sleeves pushed up to his elbows, an AK-47 in one hand, the man had a cloth covering his face; only his eyes were visible. Capt. Chauhan gripped his rifle and, in one smooth move, aimed at the figure.

'Don't make that mistake, *miyan*,' said the man as he walked towards Capt. Chauhan, casually pointing to the band of terrorists with his gun. Each one of them had their guns aimed at Capt. Chauhan already, fingers on triggers. 'I've waited all these months and I've come all this way with only one wish: to meet you in person, not to fight with you.'

'Who are you?' Capt. Chauhan demanded.

'Don't you recognize me?' the man sounded incredulous, and then chuckled. He continued to walk towards Capt. Chauhan like he had absolutely no respect for, or fear of, the gun the captain was holding. He stopped only when he was about ten metres away. He cocked his head to a side and adjusted his AK-47, his glassy eyes taking in Capt. Chauhan.

'I asked, who are you?' Capt. Chauhan demanded again.

The man laughed a bitter laugh. 'I am a fan of your talents and you don't even know who I am? *Tch, tch*!' He tapped his weapon nonchalantly, and then slowly removed the cloth covering his face.

When Capt. Chauhan saw who it was, he felt a mix of two emotions: on one hand, the unsettling feeling he'd had about this mission from the moment he laid eyes on the two intruders took form in hard facts and information in his mind like a puzzle that had been solved. And on the other, he was somewhat taken aback by the enormity of the situation unfolding before him.

He let the information sink in—he was standing in the presence of the notorious terrorist chief of LeT.

In all the articles and news items written about him when he took over Lashkar, he was described as the most ruthless terrorist seen in a long time, not only because he was a trained soldier and extremely radical in thought, but also because he was new-age and tech-savvy. According to reports, he had been a bright student who had completed his degree in engineering from a reputed college in the US, where he had apparently confided to a few batchmates about his dream of a *mujahid*-free world, and that he felt it was his destiny to make this a reality. He had then returned to his country and joined Lashkar about a decade ago, to fulfil this destiny. He had moved up the ranks pretty quickly. Khayyam was known to always think dispassionately and strategically. He was also skilled in technology and advanced warfare.

In his head, Capt. Chauhan was trying to make sense of the situation. Yes, they had suspected that Khayyam would want to take revenge for his young brother's untimely death, which is why the Indian authorities took precautionary measures and kept Capt. Chauhan out of the area for a while. But then, there had been no solid, action-worthy intelligence about trouble brewing. And yet, here they were.

In that moment, it was clear to Capt. Chauhan that Lashkar had managed to orchestrate this elaborate ambush with the sole aim of avenging Khayyam's brother's death. Neither religion nor territory had anything to do with it. Also, the terror organization had managed to keep the entire plan under the radar and away from Indian intelligence. There had been absolutely no indication that not only had Capt. Chauhan's identity been compromised, but Khayyam had also been tracking him closely enough to lure him out with a cunning plan like this.

It was clear to Capt. Chauhan that he wasn't getting out of this alive; but saving his commandoes was his highest priority, his *param dharam*, and Capt. Chauhan knew he had to do something to help his squad.

'If you want to speak to me about how your brother died, you'll have to let my soldiers go,' Capt. Chauhan said in a level voice.

Khayyam turned slowly towards the two wounded soldiers, pointing the barrel of his AK-47 towards them.

'These soldiers?' he asked.

And before Capt. Chauhan could respond, Khayyam shot them both at point-blank range. It happened in a split second, before Capt. Chauhan could even blink. He stared at the now limp bodies of his brave teammates; even though the trained soldier in him had had an inkling that this was a dire possibility, he still couldn't believe what he had just witnessed.

'What happened, Chauhan *miyan*. I let them go on your request only.'

Capt. Chauhan leaped towards Khayyam. 'I swear by my God, I will kill you like your brother was killed . . .' he yelled.

In a matter of seconds, one of Khayyam's men had clubbed Capt. Chauhan on the head with the butt of this gun, and four others had surrounded him. Capt. Chauhan fell down with the impact, but he knew that this was his chance. Scrambling into action at lightning speed, he fired his AK-47, aiming for as many terrorists as he could, before he was physically overpowered. Within seconds, three terrorists grabbed hold of Capt. Chauhan, while another hurried over to check on those whom he had shot. To Capt. Chauhan, it seemed like he had taken down, or at least injured, three of Khayyam's henchmen.

Wholly unaffected and unmoved by the struggle, Khayyam drew close, still walking leisurely, eyes gleaming. Tilting his head to a side, he studied Capt. Chauhan's face. He then crouched down beside Capt. Chauhan, who was struggling with the three terrorists holding him down, and an eerie silence took over like a thick fog.

Slowly, Khayyam ran a hand over Chauhan's face. The gesture, although intimate in theory, screamed of hatred and rage. The forest around them grew quieter.

At last, Khayyam's voice cut the silence like a whip, 'You shot my little brother, who was like a son to me. But you won't get a quick and easy death like he did.'

Capt. Chauhan knew that this was it for him. He felt the warm embrace of death like an old friend slowly taking him in. He was not afraid, in fact far from it. The Para SF commando in him refused to be scared in his final moments. Instead, in a swift move, he elbowed the man, who, in addition to holding him in a firm grip from behind, had his knee pressed into the small of the captain's back. In that brief moment of his captor's disorientation, the captain grabbed the rifle resting on the ground and hit Khayyam with all the force he could muster in this compromised state.

The sharp knife at the end of the gun hit Khayyam in the face, tearing the skin above his left eye. Blood spurted from the wound.

Capt. Chauhan, now with even more knees and boots pressing into his back and forcing him down, glared at Khayyam, his gaze level. Khayyam wiped away the blood with the cloth that had previously covered his face. 'I will remove your eyes before I kill you,' he said.

The wind whistled and escaped the area as if on cue.

* * *

By the time the Indian Army support team arrived on the spot, the terrorists had escaped, leaving behind a pile of dead bodies. The Indian team found two Para SF commandoes, still gagged and tied with nylon ropes, shot at close range; the dead bodies of three terrorists, the ones whom Capt. Chauhan had taken down; and the brutally mutilated body of Capt. Chauhan himself.

They also found Naik Manoj Kumar, who had collapsed in the foliage due to excessive blood loss. While moving away from his position on Capt. Chauhan's orders, Naik Manoj had managed to reach a point amidst the trees from where he had been able to witness what went down. He had stayed still, waiting for the right time to provide support, but just as Khayyam bent down to whisper something menacingly to Capt. Chauhan, Naik Manoj's head had drooped against his will and his eyes had closed in a dead faint. The last thing he remembered was feeling the bandage which he had fastened around his wound; it was dripping with hot blood.

Lance Naik Siddhu had only been able to make it back after the jihadis had left. After he had carried Naik Kishore bhai to safety, a heavy fog had descended like a blanket over the mountainside, and Siddhu had lost his bearings in the woods. Now, he kneeled beside the body of Capt. Chauhan—whatever was left of it—and sobbed. How he wished he had stayed with his saab, or had gone with him, doing his duty and fighting for his country until his last breath.

The Para SF squad that was sent as a part of the reinforcement team was led by Capt. Vikram Rana.

Capt. Chauhan was not only a brother-officer to Capt. Rana, but the latter also considered him his younger brother. Ever since Capt. Chauhan was posted to the same Para SF unit, Capt. Rana had taken him under his wing, and they had become very close. They were friends who shared offence strategies and discussed their travel plans for annual leave. Their sheds were adjacent to each other's in this new location in Kupwara. Amidst encounters, patrols and recces, they were family to each other. In fact, just a few hours ago, Capt. Rana had promised a worried Meera that he would have Ranvijay call her back by lunchtime. Rana had assumed this was to be a standard operation involving two rookie terror trainees, right? Capt. Rana was sure that Ranvijay would be back to the unit location by lunch, sharing tactical learnings from his latest mission.

But he was here.

It was Capt. Rana who collected Capt. Chauhan's body parts from the area, minus the eyeballs which had been gouged out of their sockets.

How did Khayyam know Ranvijay's identity? Capt. Rana wondered. Stringent measures had been taken to keep his identity secret and as far as Indian Army and intelligence knew, it had worked. But the fact that Ranvijay had been brutally tortured in what seemed like a personal vendetta more than mere retaliation during a counterterrorism mission, indicated that, not only had Ranvijay's identity been compromised, but that Khayyam and his terrorist army had also been tracking Ranvijay ever since he had been sent to Jammu through the locations to which their Para SF unit had been posted. Capt. Rana let the knowledge wash over him like a huge wave; it became clear to him that, all along, Khayyam had been patiently planning to lure Ranvijay out, without a trace of this dastardly plot on any of India's intelligence networks. And what was worse, Khayyam had done all this on Indian soil.

As silent tears of white-hot rage and sadness filled Capt. Rana's eyes, two things became eminently clear to him: the fact that Khayyam had exacted his ruthless revenge on Indian soil would boost the terrorist's confidence; and that this was a major intelligence lapse on the Indian side.

* * *

The bodies arrived at the unit location, and not one soldier could sleep that night. As Naik Manoj Kumar gave his eye-witness account of what had happened and how valiantly Capt. Chauhan had faced the terrorists, trying to save his squad members, there was not one dry eye at the assembly.

A month later, the Indian defence ministry released a statement admitting it was an intelligence failure. The signals of Lashkar's plan had been captured on the network, but these particular signals were highly encrypted using advanced coding that required time and the right assets to interpret them in time. The ministry also observed that the Indian Army needed more skillsets in decoding signals, and pledged to focus on sturdy and cutting-edge intelligence technology for the forces. The terrorists had grown tech-savvy; the army had to be one step ahead.

6

December 2019

'It feels familiar at the same time,' Lt Chauhan said in a voice that felt haunting to Maj. Rana.

He turned to look at the young lieutenant's face and felt proud. Simultaneously he felt the same white-hot rage that had surged through him all those years ago on a lonely mountainside, collecting the body parts of his beloved and brave brother officer, in this very area. Nodding towards the young officer in understanding, he turned back to face the road ahead.

The rest of the journey was spent in silence. The convoy steadily ascended the mountain and the snow kept getting thicker. After a while, they arrived at a heavily guarded barricade. Armed soldiers stood outside, ready for action, their eyes on the incoming motorcade.

The vehicles were checked, ID cards scanned, and movement orders inspected before they were allowed to enter. As soon as they were inside, the Gypsy headed straight to the makeshift office where the commanding officer was at the moment.

When their Gypsy had stopped, Maj. Rana climbed out of the vehicle and said, 'Welcome to your first high-alti, high-impact mission, Lieutenant.'

'Thank you, sir!' Lt Chauhan replied in the high-pitched voice taught in the academy, despite the nerves.

Once again, Maj. Rana felt a pang in his chest. His face shone with pride and he felt overwhelmed not just by the presence of this young and determined officer, but also because of the location: Kupwara. Maj. Rana had served several postings in the valley, including this particular area; and here he was, again.

Like the young Lt Chauhan, Maj. Rana was also glad to be on this mission, and had punched the air in elation when he found out that he had been picked, not only to be a part of it, but to lead it.

Ever since that fateful day when Maj. Rana had set out to the nearby forest range to provide backup to Capt. Chauhan's squad, he had been a changed man. Already a trained commando who had finished at the top of his class, Maj. Rana dedicated his life more than ever to bringing justice to those who planned to perpetrate terror in the area. All Para SF commandoes are feared alike by the jihadis, but Maj. Rana had relentlessly and successfully led several counterinsurgency missions in the troubled area and had earned a reputation of being driven by the loss of his brother-officer whose mutilated body parts he had collected with his own hands.

'Maj. Rana goes out on anti-terror missions prepared to die,' was what the soldiers of the paltan often said about him, with pride. 'All of us also want to avenge Capt. Chauhan's murder, but for Maj. Rana, it is his one and only motive.'

Maj. Rana knew that the time had come—he could feel it in the freezing wind around him, he could feel it in his bones. This was the opportunity he had prayed for ever since Capt. Chauhan's murder; this would get him what he wanted the most—payback. He wanted to avenge Ranvijay more than anything he had ever wanted.

Meanwhile, Lt Chauhan took a deep breath. This was it. This was the place. The young lieutenant had been in the area for the past three days but had come to this station for the first time, and it felt overwhelming.

'Jai Hind, saab!' the smart salute of the JCO, who had come out to receive the two officers, brought a proud smile to Lt Chauhan's face. Returning the salute, Lt Chauhan walked with Maj. Rana towards the CO's tent office. The nerves that were there a few minutes ago had disappeared and confidence had taken its place.

In the short distance to the CO's tent, Lt Chauhan took off the combat cap to readjust it after the long road journey and long, dark hair cascaded down around her shoulders as her hair came undone. Tucking the cap under her arm, Meera—wife of late Capt. Ranvijay Chauhan, and now known as Lt Chauhan—gathered her hair back into a tight bun and replaced her combat cap.

Look at me, she thought, *finally here.*

Finally.

* * *

Soon, the two officers were inside the commanding officer's tent.

The CO and the paltan's current 2IC, Lt Col Tariq Ahmed, Sena Medal, who had also served with and been Capt. Chauhan's senior brother officer, welcomed them.

'This is it. This is what the academy trained you for and the ministry hoped for when they selected you for the special M.I. branch,' said the CO, Col Vishwanath Iyer, Shaurya Chakra, Sena Medal. 'This is what you dreamed about, Lt Chauhan.'

'Yes, sir!' Lt Chauhan said in the same high-pitched tone she had used earlier; it was reserved for addressing seniors and giving commands in the forces.

'I am proud to have the first woman officer at this altitude in the history of the Indian Army,' said the CO. 'Since the signal was intercepted last month, a lot of hard work has gone into the planning and has led all of us in the paltan to this distinctive moment, Lt Chauhan. Your hard work and determination were what mattered the most to get us all here, in the end.'

'Sir.'

'Not only did Lt Chauhan decode the deeply encrypted, five-layered data—which the CIA boasts they're the only ones able to crack—she went above and beyond her call of duty to cleverly identify other, seemingly unrelated pieces of intel in the overlapping timeline and across varied mediums, linked them to this encrypted data and predicted—*this*!' said the CO to his 2IC. Both the senior officers looked very proud of what Meera had accomplished, because it meant a great deal for the entire unit.

'Encrypted signals sent via radio frequency, over cryptic mobile phone calls, on-ground network and more. It's impressive how Lt Chauhan put those individual pieces of intel and unrelated signals together, because the connection was not obvious at all. They didn't seem like parts of one puzzle, Ahmed—the ministry has never seen anything like this. Also, Lt Chauhan showed commendable intellect, skill and determination by connecting them, and as unusual as it seemed at first to all higher-ups in the North Block, I was informed that the ministry was amazed when she presented her findings—putting all the pieces together to form one picture that gave us one of the most solid intel in the recent past.'

Meera was still standing at attention in the presence of her commanding officer, along with two seniors. Pride in what she had accomplished, excitement, fear—not a flicker of any emotion crossed her face. To be honest, she wasn't feeling any heavy emotion at the moment, and this was certainly not the time for personal pride. From the moment she had found out she was being sent to Kupwara region, to be attached with Ranvijay's Para SF paltan, to be a part of this counterterrorism, counterinsurgency operation, her sole focus was the success of this mission. She realized that things had to go perfectly to plan, or this would all be a massive blow in multiple ways.

'You have to know, Lt Chauhan, that this is a matter of personal joy and pride for me, for all of us,' the CO said to her.

Col Vishwanath Iyer was usually a calm and collected man, whose mere presence commanded respect and instilled fear. As a Para SF commanding officer, he had led the paltan from the front for numerous counter-terror ops and tactical strikes, and was known to be almost uncannily tranquil in the face of the nastiest danger—that is how he motivated his soldiers, practising what he preached and setting an example to his regiment, that there was nothing that terrorists could do that could throw a Para SF commando off his game, off his mission, off his supreme duty. Needless to say, he was an inspiration to many young commandoes. But, ever since the previous evening, when he had got the call about Meera's intelligence report and the course of action that the HQ along with the defence ministry had planned, based on her findings, everyone in the paltan could see that the CO was not himself.

Col Iyer had been the second in command of this very paltan in April 2014 when Capt. Ranvijay was killed in action, and now he felt that, at long last, the paltan's collective ambition to avenge Ranvijay's murder stood a solid chance of becoming a reality. His hands shook in anticipation as he put them into the pockets of his combat jacket. *Finally*, he thought.

Col Iyer looked around at the sea of eager faces before him; Lt Col Ahmed beamed as he stood holding the file that contained the names of the commandoes who were selected for this mission; Lt Meera Chauhan was still standing at attention looking dead serious; and Maj. Rana standing beside her with a do-or-die expression on his face.

The CO knew exactly how Lt Col Ahmed and Maj. Rana felt; he knew that all officers and soldiers in the paltan shared that feeling. The paltan was raring to go on this mission, to avenge the blood of one of their own! *Nothing motivates like raw emotions, and all credit went to this determined and feisty young girl right here*, he thought with pride.

* * *

Meera was a signals officer, currently working with a small experimental team under the Military Intelligence— M.I.—arm of the Indian Army, that had been assigned to work on pieces of signals that were intercepted, collected or discovered by Indian intelligence agencies from various frequencies, mediums and modes. Terror organizations had evolved, and the use of enhanced technology in communication was something that was in turn pushing the Indian government to deploy more advanced machinery and far superior skillsets in intelligence. The Indian government was continuously upping the bar to keep up with this demand—Meera was one example of this. In the age of hi-tech and electronic warfare, Meera was part of an effort by the Indian government to improve the country's intelligence competencies.

As an IT engineer, specializing in hacking, and possessing an indomitable spirit, which had been revealed during her academy training, Meera was part of the special delegation trained to provide that extra edge to army intelligence crucial to keep its territory safe from the technological warfare manoeuvres that the enemy had adopted. It was also noted that, while most cadets who are trained at the various defence academies are brave and courageous, Meera's motivation was heightened by her personal tragedy. She was here to honour her husband's legacy, to make his purpose her own. And nothing drives and fuels a person more than love that has turned into grief.

In just a few months, Meera had accomplished what the army had hoped for from this advanced-technology-equipped, highly trained and high-performance team.

Meera was given an isolated piece of signal that had been picked up by Indian intelligence over radio frequency intercepted in Baramulla region—a hotbed of terrorism—and she had been able to decode it quickly. It was a cryptic voice message containing just one name, and the Indian intelligence didn't have a record under that name.

Why would someone go through all the trouble of encoding a message which had just one name? Meera wondered. She mulled over it for hours after she had passed on her findings to HQ, because this particular signal didn't make much sense—it was just a name with no background or record—it was not marked as a high priority intel, but it kept Meera up late into the night.

The radio message was comprised of just one, solitary name—and yet, it was encoded. *Why?*

And then it dawned on her! Of course, it didn't make sense *on its own* because it was just one part of a larger message.

She spoke to HQ about her findings and also told them that she believed that the encrypted name was part of a longer message which was probably being relayed in fragments. Meera wanted to pursue it, to try to look for other signals that would help uncover the entire message.

She of all people knew the disaster an intelligence failure could lead to, and she didn't want to make any mistakes or leave any stone unturned.

However, the army operates on trust that is an outcome of strict command and authority—one simply didn't neglect duty or ignore orders to follow an instinct. So, Meera had to formally apply for permission to work on this particular piece, post her assigned tasks. Maybe it was because Meera was at the right place at the right time and also because this new division of the M.I. was critical to Indian intelligence, she was promptly granted permission.

The next few days went by in a whirl of activity for Meera. She studied the piece of information which she had extracted from the encrypted signal again. She then assigned a time frame to define her research and process. Her obsessive studying of the Kashmir valley before joining the army, and of its sociopolitical nature came in handy here, and she was able to determine that the larger message would have been transmitted as recently as the last twenty to twenty-five days, not before, because of the announcement of elections in the valley—as had been the pattern since the last two election terms. Then, the heavy lifting began—collaborating with the various arms and teams across the nation, digging out pieces of information from the different channels within the defined deadline, patching together intel reports received by the Indian forces from their robust on-ground network, culling out scraps of intelligence that were processed by other divisions and teams that had a similar indicator, and poring over reports that had been filed with the tag: 'Inconclusive'.

For the next four days, Meera worked with signals intercepted by various Indian intelligence agencies across the different mediums, including radio signals that had been snagged by fluke, cryptic phone calls over the mobile network that had been flagged up by the on-ground informer network of not just the army but also the J&K Police, and encrypted messages broadcasted on public radio frequencies. By the end of the fourth day, she had uncovered five more names that were disseminated not just within Kashmir, but to locations across the board in India, emanating from one source in the Baramulla area. Including the first name that she had decoded, she now had six names—of which four were on-record with the Indian ministry, classified as category A++ terrorists by India.

This was huge, and Meera was provided immediate support and manpower to enable her investigations. Two highly trained radio operators were assigned to her on the fifth day, and she put them on the job of monitoring electromagnetic signals in the Baramulla and Kupwara area because the places were adjacent to each other and both regions had a history of being a hotbed for terrorism. Baramulla district was towards the south of Kupwara, with POK to the north and west. Kupwara was also where Ranvijay was murdered, reinforcing the knowledge that the terrorists knew this terrain like the back of their hands. Meera thought it was important to extend the area to cover both the districts.

As the team quickly stepped in and began to intercept signals from the area, Meera had time to explore some other, slightly less conventional methods of her intelligence training across her hacking course during engineering, her time at Infosys's defence wing and her special training at the academy—and put it all together to follow her gut. She had been reading about vital information being passed around the world completely undetected via the Internet, using platforms and apps that were not encrypted, and she knew the recent surge in online gaming indicated that un-encrypted gaming apps could be one such viable platform. Now, she wanted to test her theory.

The in-game chat facility was already common in many popular video games, and the feature was meant to help create a better player experience and was crucial to craft a winning strategy with your teammates in certain multiplayer games. At the same time, these chat rooms were not secure, and hence they were fast becoming not just a hunting ground for predators and fraudsters, but also the preferred medium for anti-national elements to plot, coordinate and execute their plans inconspicuously. This was not in any books or taught in any class—but Meera was sure that there were new, undetected channels of exchanging information other than the usual mediums they routinely tracked. That day, Meera set out to access, filter and identify if there was any related sensitive information being relayed through online gaming. She went through a wide variety of apps and games before discovering an extremely popular and controversial FPS—First Person Shooting—mobile game that had a robust live-chat feature which was completely free of any sort of cyber-security, so the chats there flew under the radar. With servers located in China—far from the control of the Indian government—

and the option to chat within a closed group as opposed to a public chat, this FPS game app seemed to be an ideal channel to pass illicit information.

Setting up her system to cull out information from this game app, using signatures and patterns similar to the other piece of intel that she had cracked, Meera knew she was close. She felt the anticipation build up in her bones. She had taken the initiative. She had put in the hard work. And early in the morning of day six, the puzzle clicked together.

Trembling with nervous energy, and not caring that it was 3.45 a.m., Meera passed on the vital information at once. After all, her discovery was of grave importance. And it also provided the Indian defence the ability to deliver a blow for which they had been patiently waiting and hoping.

Her breakthrough was monumental—four top leaders of Lashkar, based in Kashmir, and classified as Cat-A++ terrorists by India, and two unidentified individuals who were not on the radar of Indian intelligence, based in West Bengal and Punjab respectively, were planning a rendezvous in a small establishment on a hill above the village Keran in Kupwara district of Jammu and Kashmir, India. Keran, located on the banks of the river Kishanganga, lay on the Line of Control.

The hillside was a small, quiet and historically non-problematic area inhabited by seasonal shepherds only for a few months a year, with no more than thirty makeshift huts and kuccha houses. The area had thick, forest cover on two sides, a ridge on the third and the river Kishanganga on the fourth.

More chats were deciphered by Meera, the entire M.I. team working with her now—this was now a matter of top priority and Meera was spearheading the investigation. They revealed that the chilling agenda of the meeting between Lashkar's top brass was to finalize the organization's list of Black Operations in the valley, aiming at maximum civilian causalities. Black Ops were covert operations that were not attributable to the organization performing them, so it was clear to Meera that Lashkar would not claim responsibility for the series of brutal attacks they would finalize during this pow-wow, and that it would definitely lead to something more deadly because of global unaccountability.

The most crucial part of the information which Meera uncovered was that this covert conference was going to be chaired by none other than the Cat-A++ terrorist, one of the Indian Army's most-wanted criminals, the elusive Khayyam Anwar. He was the seventh terrorist who was not only going to be there to meet the six Lashkar leaders personally, but was also their supreme leader and planner.

Reports of Lashkar working on strengthening their cadres and expanding their terror portfolio had been rife in the valley over the past several months, and this information fit in well with Khayyam's strategic leadership vision for the group.

And all this was going to happen in less than a week.

The revelation alerted the Indian defence ministry to plan a strike. There was no other way—they could not afford to sit on their hands and do nothing.

Meera was assigned to this mission immediately, as the signals resource dedicated to intelligence. Her job would be to monitor any development on the plans, and she was asked to move closer to the area the very next day. Details of the operation were not shared with her, of course, but she knew that there was, in fact, a plot afoot for something far bigger and much bolder. As the only person who not only knew the entire message in the transmission, but could also decipher any new information concerned and/or connected to this event most efficiently, Meera was proud to be a part of the actual action plan in whatever capacity possible. It was true that the army wanted revenge, but she wanted it more. And, ably assisted by the same soldiers who were assigned to her earlier in this process, she was determined to do her job of monitoring any developments or implementing any last-minute changes to the plan, to the best of her capabilities.

Then, just yesterday the signal had come to her—she was to be attached to the special forces unit selected to execute the attack mission against Lashkar terrorists on Indian soil. She wasn't really surprised to discover that it was Ranvijay's Para SF unit, the same paltan that had paid for Khayyam's bone-chilling vengeance against one of their finest just a few years ago—the burden of which was still evident in the hunger of every officer and soldier of the formation.

The defence ministry decided to give the same unit the opportunity to avenge Ranvijay's murder. The top brass believed that, in addition to their strong terrain knowledge, unmatched combat skills and extensive counterterrorism/counter-intelligence experience, this group of special forces paratroopers had one more distinct advantage—their *jazba*, their burning desire to avenge the blood of their own. If successful, it would be poetic justice for the irreparable loss suffered by this legendary Para SF unit of commandoes.

However, Meera didn't let herself dwell on the melodramatic aspects, especially revenge; not just yet. She remained focused on delivering her best work and doing her part in making this mission a success. Not once, in the blur of the past few days, had she let herself get carried away by puerile daydreams of exacting vengeance, à la Bollywood, on the murderer of her brave husband, her beloved Ranvijay. And yet, here she was, about to set out on their mission, standing in a tent alongside the eminently competent commandoes, all of whom were equally hungry for that revenge. *This feels like a scene from someone else's life*, Meera thought for a second before hauling herself back to the present moment, blocking out the flood of emotions that would inundate her if she let them.

* * *

In the CO's tent, Maj. Rana asked for permission to speak and after a nod from Col Iyer, he began. 'The CO is right, Lt Chauhan. What you did was very impressive.'

'Absolutely right, Rana. You have made us all proud, ma'am,' agreed the CO, and then corrected himself hurriedly, 'I mean, Lt Chauhan . . .'

The CO had always addressed Meera as 'ma'am', as per army traditions. Col Iyer had remained in constant touch with Meera over the past few years, ever since Ranvijay's martyrdom, and had done his best to not only provide guidance while she was at the academy, but also motivate her on the tough days. All through these years, he continued to address Meera as 'ma'am', in the manner that all army officers address army wives. But now, she was an officer attached to the Para SF unit he was commanding, and here he was, inadvertently addressing her as 'ma'am'. Some habits are hard to break.

'It's Meera, sir, please,' Lt Chauhan prompted in a gentle voice. She was aware of the possible confusion in the CO's head and wanted to make it easier for everyone here because she felt that she had a longstanding relationship with not just the officers in this tent, but with the entire paltan—united in their grief.

The CO nodded, 'The terror camps have evolved, ever since Khayyam Anwar took over the reins. They're no longer just a bunch of brainwashed suicide bombers— their tactics have matured; their moves are more and more strategic, hitting at our weakest spots and targeting more civilians with each terror plan. And what's been most concerning is that Lashkar intel has been an elusive thing ever since Khayyam took over. They fly under the radar most of the time, avoiding both our informer network and our intelligence signals.'

'Sir,' Meera nodded in agreement, and added, 'this one message, being relayed over a span of three weeks in the form of advanced and clever bits and pieces of code across various channels and mediums, camouflaged under layers of sophisticated encryption, is an example of their tech progress, sir.'

Col Iyer walked over to the three officers. 'God knows how many more tech advancements we're up against. We need to be well prepared. Nothing can go wrong with this one, Rana.'

Maj. Rana nodded. He knew that a few aspects of the mission were still being fine-tuned, but one thing was clear to Col Iyer, to himself and to the other commandoes who had been hand-picked for this mission: justice would prevail for this Para SF unit within the next twenty-four hours.

'We got the go-ahead from the defence ministry early this morning, relayed to us by HQ. They're going to be monitoring this closely.' Col Iyer picked up a file from the desk behind him and passed it over to Meera.

'Prepare for your first active combat field mission, Lt Meera. We leave at 3 a.m. tomorrow,' said the CO, 'and if your intel is right, Khayyam won't know what hit him.'

Meera nodded, and after a sharp salute to the CO and the 2IC, she marched out of the tent alongside Maj. Rana.

There was turmoil inside her. Despite having decoded the signals, despite being the first lady officer to be cleared for a combat mission in this area, she wasn't going to be at the forefront. Yes, she was a part of the Para SF squad that had been assigned to the mission, based on the intel she had deciphered, but everyone in a mission squad has a specific duty, and she had been told that hers was to track radio signals in the area during the mission. So, she would not be involved in the actual combat on the top of the hill, the location she had been able to pinpoint after her deep dives into the encrypted signals. Instead, she and the two operators, assigned to assist her with intercepting and decoding signals, would be stationed at the outermost periphery of the operation, at the very edge of where the action was going to be, behind a line of trees and inside a makeshift hut, playing their small part of the overall huge job.

That was the way it worked.

Every commando assigned to this mission had been carefully picked by Col Iyer, Lt Col Ahmed and Maj. Rana. The squad included Ranvijay's combat buddy, Havaldar Siddhu, among other commandoes who had fought alongside Ranvijay in the valley. Every soldier on this mission had a specific task and together they worked like a well-oiled machine that completed every mission successfully. Bursting blindly into a terrorist's lair without much knowledge of the arms and ammunition they wielded, was a dangerous thing to do, to say the least. Therefore, this operation was being led by the commando officer who not only had extensive experience in the terrain, he was an on-the-ground war-tactics expert to boot—Maj. Rana. Meera knew that being on a mission spearheaded by him was an honour and a privilege.

Meera knew how badly Maj. Rana wanted to eliminate Khayyam Anwar, and she also realized that with him at the helm, this mission was bound to be successful—provided her intel was bang on, and that she was able to track any last-minute changes in the plan, if any.

She was elated to be a part of this mission, in whatever capacity—big or small—that was set to bring down Ranvijay's assassin. And then there was also her absolute conviction that Maj. Rana was going to do everything in his power to get justice for Ranvijay. But was it going to be enough for Meera?

7

Outside the CO's tent, Meera looked around at the snow-clad turf and time seemed to freeze for her as she let herself think about how fast things had changed over the last few hours, and how many emotions she had experienced twisting inside her.

Just a few days ago, when she had discovered that she was being deployed to Kupwara to be a part of this CI/CT mission, she had almost gone into shock.

And then, when she found out what her role was going to be in the operation, Meera had tried to reason with herself and come to terms with the insignificant, background role to which she had been relegated.

This is more than enough, she said to herself multiple times.

This *should* be enough.

I'm going to be a part of the massive operation that will bring Khayyam down—I will have a hand in his downfall, she told herself repeatedly.

However, owing to her inherent feisty nature, deep down, she obviously wanted more. She wanted to be one of the commandoes on the frontline. Nothing else was going to be enough. But Para SF didn't have women in active combat yet, so, for now, she had no option but to take what she got—while recognizing that the Indian Army had given her a chance of a lifetime.

That fire in her that Ranvijay had recognized and loved, wanted her to be the one to put the first and the final bullet in Khayyam's head—but this yearning to understand its boundaries at this time. It was one thing to stay awake for nights on end, telephoning various intel units across Northern Command to collect fragmented signals, navigating through tons of data to put the pieces of a baffling puzzle together, but it was an entirely different thing to hope for a ringside seat at the climax. This was real life, this was the Indian Army and there were rules to follow—not only for your own sake, but for your troops' and for the overall success of the operation.

Meera knew this, of course. She knew that she had joined the army after Ranvijay's murder not just to honour him and his life, but to also carry forward his dream of doing his bit to build a safe country where the citizens could sleep peacefully at night, where no intruder with harmful intentions would go undetected and where no plans of terror would unfold.

Ranvijay had often talked about how he disliked the God-like portrayal of soldiers like him in the media. He thought it made soldiers seem like a segmented fantasy invoked only on Republic Day or Independence Day or

when something unfortunate happened on the borders—
and this portrayal also made people easily forget these heroes
when the context died or was taken over by something else
that was more newsworthy.

'We are normal people, with families to take care of,
bills to pay and plans of going on a stress-free, lazy vacation
to Maldives after saving enough money from our *sarkari*
salary,' he would say to Meera. 'A soldier is not God-like;
he's human with dreams and has a job to do like everyone
else. The only thing that makes a soldier stand apart from
the rest is the willingness to stand for something bigger
than himself. It's the devotion to duty and the desire to
safeguard the life of his troops and his people that makes
the soldier bigger than his circumstances. And if everyone
realized this, it would be a better world.'

Meera often pondered over the idea of standing up
for something that was bigger than her personal goals and
personal desires—like the burning desire to kill Khayyam
herself. Up until now, when annihilating Khayyam had
seemed like a far-fetched fantasy, she knew that the
nation and Ranvijay's legacy took precedence over her
own desires. But now that her goal was within reach, she
needed to recalibrate her beliefs and ambitions. Under any
other circumstance, she would've been happy and content
just being part of a combative CI/CT mission, the first for
a lady officer—she was making history here!

However, this was too close home. She kept
dwelling on the way Khayyam had personally wreaked
his vengeance on Ranvijay, inhumanely torturing and
mutilating his victim's body—how could Meera not hope

to exact the same vengeance from him, if not more, now that she had been instrumental in pinning down the elusive, deceptive bastard?

Moreover, after murdering Capt. Chauhan, Khayyam had amassed huge support from separatists, and—fuelled by confidence—a bigger appetite for terror on Indian soil. He was almost untouchable now—never being directly involved but always omnipresent in every strategically planned and vicious terror attack by the Lashkar in the valley. He had killed a lot more innocent people since then.

This had been a tough battle in Meera's heart and mind at the time. She knew she had to keep the emotions at bay for this one. There would be time enough to break down and cry, but that time was not now—not until she had done her job well and the squad had emerged successful at the end.

Because, let's face it, it wasn't just about the seven ruthless jihadi terrorist leaders who were going to be at the location, if Meera's analysis was correct, this was Khayyam Anwar they were trying to eliminate.

Not apprehend.

Eliminate.

At the same time, she also knew the raw, uncomfortable truth about herself, that, given the opportunity, she would do anything, even bypass any order, to kill Khayyam herself.

The chilly wind picked up, jolting Meera back to the present time. Pulling up the collars of her combat jacket to cover her ears, Meera looked at Maj. Rana. He stood still, stoically facing the wind, hands in his pockets, gazing at the white scenery. Then he turned towards her.

'Even though there's almost four to five feet of snow in this area right now,' he said to Meera, 'the river Kishanganga doesn't freeze.'

Meera nodded.

'The water is ice cold at all times in that river, even more so right now, but it is flowing and the current is strong,' Maj. Rana continued.

'We'll need to ensure no one escapes,' replied Meera because she understood what he was driving at. It was going to be difficult to carry out a search operation in a fast-flowing, ice-cold river along the LOC, especially with POK on the opposite bank.

'Let's study the satellite images again,' suggested Maj. Rana, walking towards a row of sheds on the side. 'And we need to prep—these few hours will fly like minutes and 3 a.m. will be upon us before we know it.'

* * *

The squad assembled inside one of the sheds, where they would spend the next few hours preparing for the mission.

Maj. Rana explained the approach. They were going to be divided into three teams and approach the target area in a *chakravyhu* formation.

The first team, also known as the assault team, consisted of commandoes whose task was to eliminate as many terrorists as possible, as quickly as possible. They formed the innermost circle. This team would also have a fire support team to provide cover fire.

The second team, called the inner cordon, would cordon off the main points to intercept and eliminate any terrorists who managed to escape the assault team. The placement of the inner cordon team was carefully picked. The aim was to curtail all seven terrorists and their aides, if any, within the inner cordon.

The third team was called the outer cordon and was to be tactically placed like the outermost layer of a chakravyuh. Their job was to take out anyone who escaped the inner cordon and tried to flee the scene. In most Para SF CI/CT ops, there's little need for the outer cordon because the assault and inner cordon teams almost always contained the mission successfully. However, close attention was always paid to the outer cordon in terms of placing them at strategic points as per the terrain, to ensure complete success. Meera was to be a part of the outer cordon. She and the two radio-operator soldiers were going to be amongst the last and final layer of commandoes who would be placed at the edge of the forest, monitoring movement, and the three of them would also be intercepting signals in the area on their equipment.

Maj. Rana was going to be leading the assault team, and Havaldar Siddhu was the lead sniper in the supporting-fire team along with the other commandoes with a variety of long-range, medium-range and short-range weapons. Siddhu hadn't yet gathered the courage to speak to Lt Meera. What would he even say? he didn't know.

Should I apologize to her for not having been able to help Ranvijay saab that day, or should I thank her for giving us this chance by finding out about that bastard Khayyam's plan? he wondered.

After I kill the bastard, maybe I'll know what to say, he decided.

Meanwhile, oblivious to the gamut of almost tangible emotions in the shed amongst Ranvijay's friends and peers, Meera was busy getting to grips with the op strategy. Monitoring signals during this operation was highly critical because there were chances that, once trapped, the terrorist leaders would transmit distress signals over their radio devices, or even call for reinforcement.

Time passed quickly as the squad pored over the satellite images of the area which had been provided to the Para SF units directly by the ministry, because operations like these are carried out with little or no time to conduct an on-ground recce—and the recces are done on maps, including satellite images. Nevertheless, the squad needed to be familiar with the terrain to be able to cordon it off and strategically block any chances of escape.

Meera looked at one of the satellite images of the area, where she and her team had been ordered to station themselves. Taking in the edge of the thick forest where they would be positioned with the river on their right and the other minutiae in the area, she let the image embed itself in her mind. It wasn't going to be easy to be in a combat operation in a terrain that was completely unknown to her, but maps had been her friends since her academy days, and the satellite images were fairly detailed, providing her with information about the area that she knew would come in handy.

All pivotal points were covered and explained, and then it was time for Maj. Rana to order the squad to get a couple of hours of rest before they set out on their mission. Before that, however, he announced the name of this operation to the squad.

'Operation Payback,' he said, looking at the sea of faces before him. 'This is Operation Payback. I want each and every one of you to strive for the payback we deserve—that Capt. Ranvijay Chauhan deserved.'

The entire shed reverberated with the hearty 'Yes, sir!' Meera noticed that every face in that shed reflected eagerness to do their bit to get payback. Maj. Rana, together with all the commandoes, recited the Para SF war cry before setting out: 'Balidan Parma Dharma'. Hearing the chant gave Meera the chills.

She waited for a few seconds, watching the commandoes leave the shed before following them out. When she eventually stood beside Maj. Rana, he said, 'Khayyam won't know what hit him,' Maj. Rana said to her.

'No disrespect, sir; you know I am truly grateful for the chance to be a part of this mission, but I sincerely hope he *will* know what hit him. I wish we could tell him our names and who we are before we eliminate him.'

'Meera, don't . . .' a dark shadow fell over Maj. Rana's face, and he looked around to see if anyone had overheard her.

Ever since Maj. Rana had met Meera a few years ago, he had felt like she was the younger, brash and naughty sister he never had. Ranvijay had shared Rana's mobile phone number with Meera just a week after their *rishta* had been finalized, and Meera had quickly become like family to him. It helped that Rana was also a Rajput, albeit from Pune, and their family cultures were similar, making it very easy to understand each other's position between the three of them. He had attended Ranvijay and Meera's *sangeet* function and before their wedding in Bikaner; Meera had nearly convinced him to attend the wedding as team bride. If Ranvijay had not gotten quite so cross at the mere suggestion, Rana might have joined team bride for real because the sangeet had been such great fun.

At the wedding, Meera had addressed Maj. Rana as *Bhai-sa*, which meant elder brother in her Rajasthani culture, and Maj. Rana loved it. He, like Ranvijay, was an only child and while he already considered Ranvijay his younger brother, he liked the idea of Meera as his kid sister. Their relationship until Ranvijay's murder was fun and supportive, with Maj. Rana looking out for her, especially when she shifted to his hometown, Pune. But after Ranvijay's death, they became like real brother and sister to one another, providing strength to the other in times when no one else understood their pain and suffering. Over the years, their relationship developed into a strong bond. They were driven by the same motive. They had suffered the same loss, albeit different in capacity.

Capt. Rana mentored and protected Meera in a way that didn't feel patronizing or condescending to her, given her strong independence and high intelligence. That was a blessing. And right now, she was aware that he was worried about what she had just said.

'Don't worry, sir. I know the plan and am going to follow your orders to my last breath. The stark reality of the situation is setting in only now, I guess—up until here, it was all part of the job. But now, it has started to feel real.' In professional and formal set-ups, they addressed each other as protocol and hierarchy would demand.

Maj. Rana nodded in understanding (and slight relief), and fixed his gaze to the ground. After a short silence, he said, 'Ranvijay is proud of you, Lt Chauhan; wherever he is.'

'Thank you, sir,' Lt Chauhan replied, her voice ever so slightly quavering at the mention of her late husband.

This is where he gave his life; this is where I will start mine, she thought.

* * *

With just a couple of hours left for the launch of the mission, Meera sat in a shed holding the satellite images and took a deep breath. Since that fateful day when she was given that one intelligence signal to analyse, which led to this massive discovery, Meera had diligently avoided dwelling on anything that could cloud her mind or compromise her judgement with pointless emotions. Whenever she found her thoughts drifting, she would ruthlessly haul them back and refocus on the task at hand. Training the mind for victory was a skill she had learnt in the academy and had put to use often.

She had followed every instruction to the tee, and had gone the extra mile, putting in all the hard work required of her and now, here she was; she felt that, over and above her diligence and tenacity, luck had been on her side all along to bring her this far. She could now afford a small luxury and allow herself to think about what was actually happening and to feel it in her blood. The symphony of it all coming together was almost poetic in an unrealistic way. After all her struggles and difficulties, the little incidents leading up to this very moment felt too good to be true.

She did have it tough. Losing Ranvijay had been a blow that almost killed her; but it had proved to be so much worse—she had to continue living, without him, and she had not known how to do so. And then, she decided to follow in Ranvijay's footsteps and join the Indian Army. Being a part of the army was something that was both her life's purpose and paid her homage to Ranvijay's memory. She drew strength from knowing that she was on the same path that Ranvijay had trodden. She knew that her loss, no matter how much time passed, would never be assuaged, so she wanted to keep going.

She let the emotions wash over her, naming them one by one.

Excitement. *I was able to put this together. I'm here. I'm here because of my hard work and purely on merit. Ranvijay would be so proud!*

Grief. *Ranvijay. He isn't here to witness this, to hold my hand and tell me that the fire in my belly will see me through my nervousness.*

Rage. *Ranvijay isn't here any more. He was taken away from me too soon, brutally murdered by Khayyam—an animal who isn't only still at large but has killed several more since then because of his brutal agenda.*

Revenge. *I want to avenge Ranvijay, and all the other lives lost at the hands of Khayyam.*

Relief. *I am here. This is my chance to do my bit. What I do matters.*

Fear. *What if the analysis was wrong? What if, even though we had been spot on, Khayyam still manages to evade our dragnet? What if I mess up big time as the first lady officer in combat and in active ops—what if I fail?*

Anticipation. *The analysis in intelligence is not wrong. It is rock solid. And I can't wait to participate in this huge adventure. I'm not only going to contribute, in a small way, to*

*making history, I'm also getting the rare opportunity to achieve
a personal victory.*

And finally, courage. *I belong here. My work is part of
what has made this mission happen. I'm Ranvijay's warrior-
princess. I've got this.*

* * *

Two hours later, a team of fifty-one fearsome and lethal
Para SF commandoes and three Signals and M.I. officers,
including India's first woman officer in combat, set off on
the trail to Khayyam's secret rendezvous with six Lashkar
leaders.

This was a paratrooper squad. To avoid losing the
advantage of the element of surprise, helicopters had been
ruled out; the squad had, therefore, been discreetly dropped
off by army trucks about 4 km away from Keran village
and had to proceed on foot from there. Their drop had been
designed in such a way that even if someone had noticed
it, it would look like a mundane, routine drill by the Indian
Army—a regular occurrence in the area.

Each soldier was carrying approximately 40 kg,
excluding the weapon they held for quick action. The
weapons being carried by the Para SF commandoes on
this mission included the 5.56mm TAR-21 Assault Rifle,
7.62mm Sniper Rifles, AK-47s, Carl Gustav 84mm
Rocket Launchers, Grenade Launchers and 9mm pistols.
Maj. Rana's choice of weapon for close and medium range
was the fully automatic M4A1, and he carried his trusted
Assault Rifle almost reverentially. As they walked, he went
over the plan in his head once again:

Upon reaching their pre-decided locations, each team lead would confirm their positions on radio devices to Maj. Rana, and then he and his two leading commandoes would determine and confirm the presence of the terrorists at the location as per the intel, before giving the go-ahead. The assault-and-fire-support teams would simultaneously attack, upon receiving Maj. Rana's signal, and destroy the deceptive establishment of huts and makeshift houses that harboured the jihadi leaders, while the snipers in the inner cordon took out the terrorists using their silenced guns with the telescopic sights.

Maj. Rana had given clear instructions to the entire squad that the assault team and the cover-fire teams needed to attack simultaneously if they were to benefit from the element of surprise and inflict maximum damage. The rest of the inner cordon team, other than the snipers, the ones with medium- and short-range weapons needed to be on alert, ready to join in without wasting a second if required, so that not one terrorist could escape the area.

As they moved stealthily across the terrain, Maj. Rana could sense the heightened emotions of each and every one of these commandoes. High *josh* and motivation could be felt like tangible tremors in the air and yet, there was no sound except for the susurration of the cold wind.

Each one of these commandoes had been on several CI/CT missions, but they knew that the stakes were high this time. Not only was the Indian Defence Ministry directly involved in this, but they were familiar with the anguish felt by the Indian Army at large on Ranvijay's murder, and was expecting this squad to emerge successful after they collectively exacted revenge.

Meera's involvement in the intelligence report and her presence in this mission only enhanced this energy, proving to be extra motivation for the squad.

As the group moved across the terrain towards their target, Meera thought of the first time she had met Ranvijay.

I was an ignorant child back then, so naïve, she thought.

Back then, not one cell in her body had had the faintest idea that this was where she would be a few years down the line. That version of Meera seemed like a whole different person from whom she was today—although Ranvijay would have argued that it was still her in essence and that it was that same fire in the belly that had gotten her here. An unlikely place for a girl from a quiet city in Rajasthan, who thought her greatest achievement had been to score a government seat in an engineering degree. She smiled faintly—*what a life this has been*. And even if it were all to end today, it would've been worth it. Death was a very real possibility now; especially as a soldier in active combat.

Was she nervous?

She should be, one would think. This was her first CI/CT mission, a dangerous combat operation involving deadly terrorists. And while it was one thing to be a part of the Indian Army's anti-insurgency intelligence task force, working from the relative safety of an air-conditioned office in an army cantonment in a terror-free city, relying solely on her intelligence and hard work, it was a whole other thing to be crouching on Kashmiri soil with an AK-47 in one's hands, prepared to face the enemy behind the encrypted signals. Any normal person would have been nervous, to say the least.

Am I nervous? Meera asked herself. The gusting wind speeded up, as if on cue.

And then she heard Ranvijay whisper in her ears through the wind: *Yuddh hee toh veer ka praman hai* (fighting for your side in a war is proof of a brave heart).

You're right, Ranvijay, she thought. *A war is when a soldier can prove his mettle and I will prove that I'm worthy, by living through this or in my death. Either way, this mission is my yuddh.*

With this oddly comforting thought, Meera pushed the emotions away and gripped her AK-47 a little tighter as she continued to move quietly through the forest like the commandoes around her.

As the wind picked up pace, the squad also picked up theirs. They had two hours to reach their mark, and thus far, they were on track.

8

Look at me, thought Meera. Twenty years old and the first girl in her family to get into an engineering college! She had always been a bright student, keen to learn more than her curriculum and pushing her limits to achieve the best academic results. Currently, she was in her second year of the four-year engineering degree course at ECB Bikaner, pursuing a BTech degree in computer science.

ECB had not been her first choice of college, having secured a good rank in the government-run Rajasthan state engineering competitive exam; however, going out of the city had not been a possibility because, although her family was loving and nurturing, they were orthodox. While her father, the family's patriarch, had supported Meera in her education and had always taken pride in how bright his youngest was, sending away his young spinster daughter to a strange new city was where he drew the line. It isn't safe, he would say—and that was that.

He belonged to the school of thought which decreed that, while girls must definitely have a good education, they were not meant to earn a living for the household—that was a man's job. In his opinion, daughters were to be taken care of and protected, not sent out to work. He dreamed of Meera living a safe and comfortable life, married to a man he had chosen for her, the scion of a respectable family. And he even believed that the nature of her bridegroom's job—a captain in the Indian Army—would keep Meera happy and busy in setting up and running a household and meeting new people as they moved from one location to another every few years as her husband's job demanded. He had put great thought into this! And he felt understandably frustrated that Meera couldn't see his point of view. *I have thought of everything for her good; why isn't this good enough for her?* he would often wonder.

Only this morning he had stormed out of the house after a heated argument with his stubborn daughter. He had wanted her to relinquish her pointless ambition to work for a corporate. She was soon going to be a *fauji* wife, relocating every time her husband's posting changed.

She told him that various big companies would come to their college campus on a placement drive and now that she was eligible to sit for interviews, she fervently hoped 'to be placed in Infosys' and be sent to their Mysore campus by the end of her degree. This didn't make any sense to her father. What a waste of time! Why did she want a 9-to-5 job? He had ensured that she had a good future and a fulfilling life ahead of her, and he just couldn't wrap his head around her pointless rebellion. Meera's elder sister had been much more amenable to his way of thinking. She had completed her graduation in commerce before he found an eligible match for her—a solid Rajput RAS officer, who was currently posted in a powerful government administerial position in Kota—and had ensured that she had a safe, comfortable and fulfilling life. But he also knew that Meera was feisty, true to the Rajput blood coursing through her veins. After all, it was he who had jokingly nicknamed her 'Jhansi ki Raani' when she was very little because of the way she always dug her heels in.

Frustrated, he had told her that she ought to have opted for a BEd degree, which is more practical for an army wife. He regretted the words as soon as they were out, but as a man who rarely revealed his emotions, he had stormed out, leaving behind a seething Meera in the veranda. *Her mother will know how to calm her down*, he told himself.

A few hours later, Meera was sitting cross-legged on the floor of the open veranda of her home. They lived in their old ancestral house. Its floor plan was like the domiciles in India of yore with an enclosed courtyard (veranda) in the centre, open to the sky and surrounded by rooms. It had thick, sturdy walls and a flat roof for protection against the blazing summers of Rajasthan. The house had been passed down through the generations and was the only home Meera had ever known. This veranda was her sanctuary. She slept here under the stars on summer nights; and on winter evenings, she was usually the one who coaxed her strict, traditional dad to light a fire in a *tagari* for them here, as her mom cooked daal-baati over a mud *chulha*. She had played non-stop hopscotch with her friend from the neighbourhood here as a kid, had danced at her sister's wedding sangeet and then at her brother's engagement get-together on a small wooden stage which had been erected in a corner of the courtyard.

Meera knew her father meant well, she did. But she had *always* wanted more than what was available to her. And even in her understanding of her father, his old, traditional ways and his desire to provide for a cushioned life for her, she knew she had the upper hand. Because her father was stubborn, but Meera was his child indeed. Nothing could deter her.

Her mother stepped out of the kitchen, a room in a corner of the enclosed courtyard. She was in her traditional Rajasthani *poshak* and looked livid. Meera's mom hated to be caught in the crossfire of arguments between her husband and Meera.

'The two of you are made from the same mould and God knows I can't handle you both butting heads,' she grumbled, handing a big bowl of pea pods to Meera and an old newspaper. She sat down in front of her mutinous child, spread the newspaper between them and emptied the bowl on to it.

'I know what I want,' Meera shrugged, shelling the peas automatically, 'and I think I should be allowed to make my own choices in life, Ma.'

'Even if you sit for the placements this year or get recruited, of what use will any of it be because you're going to be married in a few months,' her mother sighed. 'Kuwar Saa is going to move from station to station, and you will move with him. I don't think Infosys will allow its latest employee to be on Bharat Bhraman.'

'One, he is not your Kuwar Saa yet: call him Ranvijay. And two, I can stay in the place where my job is, and he can visit me during his holidays. Why am I the one expected to move with him and not the other way around? Both of us are getting married. Why should only I have to make the sacrifices?'

Meera looked at her mother and noticed how exhausted she looked. She knew her mother only wanted what was best for her, but like Meera's dad, her mom's notions of what was best for her daughter diametrically differed from Meera's. But Meera understood, and playfully added, 'And as you said, I am going to be married soon anyway, so I'll be someone else's problem then—you don't have to worry any longer.'

'And that someone else has no idea what he's in for!' Ma said with an exaggerated sigh. Meera chuckled. Ma added, 'But I'll always worry about you, you know that. A mother always worries about the wellbeing of her children and always prays for blessings for them.'

'Yeaaahhh, but you have three kids, Ma! You can relax by the third child, I guess,' said Meera, helping herself to some of the shelled peas—they tasted so fresh and good.

'Yeaaahhh, but the elder two combined have never given me half as much grief,' Ma replied, slapping Meera's marauding hands from the peas. '*Bas kar*, I need to cook this . . .'

Meera laughed, her mouth full of the fresh and sweet green peas. 'Ranvijay is happy to let me work, by the way,' she said. 'He told me that as a Para SF officer, he's mostly going to be on field postings, and as soon as I finish my engineering, I can move to wherever my job takes me, and we'll make it work.'

'*Chalo, theek hai,*' said Ma. 'At least you'll be in the same city until you finish your degree, and I'll get to see you often.'

Ranvijay's parents were also in Bikaner so, even after their wedding, Meera would be in the same city as her parents. Ranvijay was in a field location right now, a non-family station, which worked out very well for Meera, who had two more academic years to complete.

Although theirs had been a typical arranged marriage, Ranvijay and Meera had met a few times after their engagement, which had been five months ago. It hadn't been easy, because Ranvijay was always away on postings. However, Meera made sure she sneaked in some time with Ranvijay whenever he was in town.

While arranged marriages were strictly formal affairs, meeting Ranvijay in an informal environment was crucial for Meera. She needed to know Ranvijay's views on her career plans, mainly about her completing her engineering degree, and his outlook on life in general. She knew she couldn't marry someone as orthodox as her father. She needed to be with someone who gave her the freedom to pursue her dreams and goals. Meera was also concerned that Ranvijay might be one of those dreaded army officers who expected their wives to tamely follow them around the country without any ambition of their own.

And this endeavour to meet Ranvijay informally and without the knowledge of their parents, to get to know him better, paid off. Although Ranvijay was initially shy in an adorable way, they hit it off almost immediately. Meera was happy to discover that not only was Ranvijay well educated himself—he was a Mayo Ajmer School alumni, an NDA pass out, and planned to pursue his MTech in Weaponry and War Tactics in a few years when he picked up the next rank of a Major—he was also very supportive of her studying further and following her dreams. In fact, it was a delightful surprise to Meera that Ranvijay seemed confident that she would not only have the space to follow her dream, but that she would also achieve her goals.

Having someone believe in, not just her abilities, but also in her dreams was an unaccustomed luxury to Meera. Her father loved her to bits and her ma supported her unconditionally to the best of her own capabilities, but Meera's dreams were beyond their comprehension and as a result, Meera had always felt that she had to constantly prove herself worthy of their faith in her—even if her aspirations and ambitions were fairly ordinary for a girl her age.

So, having another person have absolute faith in her felt like a dream come true. It was also a massive inspiration.

Ranvijay encouraged her to study harder and do her best and to be independent.

'Army wives need to be self-reliant, Meera,' he had said the first time they had met. Sheer music to Meera's ears, who didn't know the first thing about an army wife's life but realized that a man who mentioned this in their first candid chat was definitely worth it.

Their first unofficial meeting was something they often discussed later, mainly because of their instantaneous rapport and also because of Meera's boldness.

This is how it went: Unbeknownst to their parents, just two days after the rishta was finalized following a formal meeting with their respective parents and siblings, Meera arranged to secretly meet Ranvijay over coffee. She had decided that if she discovered that he wasn't going to be supportive of her ambitions, she'd find a way out of the rishta. Her dad would be furious of course, but she'd cross that bridge when she came to it.

She already knew that Ranvijay wasn't on any social media—she had done her due diligence. Indian Army personnel weren't allowed to be on public social platforms, but she had checked Instagram and Facebook nonetheless, just to be sure. Sliding into his DMs would've made it so easy to set up this meeting . . . *but when had her life ever been simple?* she thought with a sigh. She didn't have his personal telephone number, so she decided to steal Ranvijay's folks' landline number from her father's phone. And she did!

The next afternoon, from the privacy of her bedroom, Meera telephoned the landline number. Ranvijay's mother answered the call, and Meera pretended to be a lady soldier, calling to check up on Capt. Ranvijay Chauhan as per 'the government's orders'.

Confused, Ranvijay's mom handed him the phone.

'Hi, it's Meera,' she said the moment he said hello. 'Meera from the rishta.'

'Rishta?' Ranvijay said, sounding taken aback like he didn't know, or remember, about his wedding being finalized. The confusion in his voice immediately made Meera slightly annoyed. How many rishtas or Meeras was this guy dealing with?

'Yes. Rishta. Wedding. Shaadi. *Din shagna da,*' she said impatiently. 'Ring any bells?'

'Virat Kohli, Anushka Sharma?' Ranvijay replied. He hadn't expected Meera to call, and his mom had told him that some 'lady soldier' was on the phone for him as per sarkari orders, which hadn't made any sense. So he was understandably surprised at the beginning of the call; but after that initial second of confusion, he realized it was her. And then followed this bizarre conversation in her irritated, yet slightly nervous, voice—it made him smile.

'What . . .?'

'What?'

'Okay, yes . . . she did make her entry for the main wedding ceremony with the song. Unnecessary yet impressive pop-culture knowledge, I suppose,' Meera begrudgingly admitted.

'More like cricket knowledge. Or cricket-adjacent knowledge. Not pop culture,' Ranvijay offered.

'Whatever,' Meera rolled her eyes and then got back on topic, 'we're getting married. I mean, maybe we are . . .'

'Maybe?'

'I don't know yet . . . which is why I'm calling you.'

'So, no *din shagna da*?' Ranvijay asked light-heartedly, making Meera want to smile. But this was no time for jokes.

'Ranvijay,' she said firmly.

'Meera,' he said simply.

'Please don't say my name!' Meera whispered, suddenly more nervous than irritable. 'Just pretend you're talking to a lady soldier so that your mother doesn't suspect anything!'

'Okay, ma'am. There are no lady soldiers, by the way. Lady officers, yes. But no lady soldiers yet.'

'How unfortunate for the army,' Meera lamented.

'Absolutely,' Ranvijay agreed.

'We need to meet. I have to discuss some urgent matters with you.'

'Okay,' Ranvijay agreed immediately. 'I'm assuming this is a covert meeting?'

'Absolutely,' Meera said emphatically.

He chuckled and they decided a time to meet at a coffee shop in the city, far away from both their homes so there was no risk of running into anyone they knew.

Meera arrived a bit early at the coffee shop. She sat by herself at a table in the corner, looking at the scene before her without registering anything. She was nervous. What if Ranvijay didn't see things her way? What if, like her father, Ranvijay also believed that women needed to rely on the menfolk, or the elders, of the family for their well-being? If he didn't accept her career aspirations, this wedding could not happen, and she would have to face the wrath and disappointment of her father. Just the thought of it made her shudder.

One step at a time, she told herself. She had come here today with one goal: to inform Ranvijay about her future plans for herself, to be honest and straightforward with him and she hoped for honesty in return. But she didn't know how it would go down with Ranvijay . . . and she was anxious about the outcome.

By the time Ranvijay arrived, which was exactly five minutes before the time they had decided upon, Meera had planned for every scenario and had tried to prepare for each.

* * *

'I want to complete my engineering degree and then I want to get a job,' she said to Ranvijay as soon as they got the coffee order out of the way although the barista was still within earshot. 'My father wants me to marry and run a household, but I have ambitions; I want to do more than just be someone's wife. I want to have a career; I want to be financially independent and I want to do so much more in my life than run a household and have children.'

Ranvijay nodded, his expression deadpan. He wanted her to say what she had clearly prepared in advance to say to him; he could see how much it meant to her, and he wasn't one to interrupt a lady when she was speaking, anyway.

'I'm going to appear for my college placements next year,' Meera continued. 'And I'm hoping to get selected for Infosys—my dream company! And TCS is also coming to campus so even if Infosys does not happen, I have other options. So, you see, I'm definitely going to get placed in a big IT firm and I'm going to go wherever they send me for the job.'

Ranvijay nodded again.

'And as you too belong to a Rajput family, you know I can't rebel against my family,' Meera continued. 'But I'm afraid I can't marry you if you don't support my career ambitions. That's why I wanted to meet you today—I want to be honest from the word go and understand our expectations of each other.'

'Um, okay . . .' Ranvijay said, fascinated by this spirited girl who had reached out to invite him for this clandestine coffee rendezvous. He had always loved and admired spunk in the company he kept—part of the job of being a Para SF commando—and he loved it even more in this girl who was as bright and smart as she was beautiful.

'So, the ball is in your court, my friend,' Meera said, as the coffee arrived. 'And I would add that, if this is not your cup of tea, now is the time to say so. If you don't want me to finish my engineering and then go on to a job, I can't marry you and obviously it's going to be you who'll have to break it to our parents that we can't marry—not me.'

'And why is that?' Ranvijay had asked curiously, sipping his coffee. He was enjoying himself.

'*Because* . . .' Meera explained with the long-suffering patience of a grown-up talking to a toddler, 'obviously, I can't be the one to say no to this rishta—my dad will go ballistic, or it will be another big drama at home and God alone knows how long my ma will continue to root for me.' She sighed. 'So, I'm giving you a choice, Ranvijay. You can go home and tell your parents you can't marry me and have them talk to my dad to break off the rishta.'

'Okay, I'll tell my parents,' replied Ranvijay, a smile threatening to burst on his face.

'That you don't want to marry me?'

'That I *want* to marry you,' said Ranvijay, 'if you want to marry me, that is.'

'And what about my degree?'

'What about it? I mean, I'm assuming you'll complete it and top your batch. And then I hope Infosys recruits you, like you want, and we can both live in the Mysore campus? Is that even possible? How does that work, tell me again . . .'

'Oh my God!' Meera said before he could finish. 'Promise?' she almost jumped in excitement.

'Promise, Meera,' said Ranvijay, earnestly. 'I don't see why this should be an issue at all. I understand our traditional families and their mindsets, but what you and I do is completely up to us.'

'Seriously?'

'Yeah. I am a newly commissioned Parachute Regiment Special Forces commando, Meera. I'm going to be away a lot in the first few years of my service. I'm driven by my sworn duty to the nation—I'm willing to do what it takes to give my all. And it would make me happy to share my life with someone who's as driven and as strong as I am. And as an army wife, a woman needs to have courage and—'

He stopped mid-sentence because the look on Meera's face was something he hadn't seen till now. She looked . . . flushed.

Meera was turning red because this was the first time since the wedding discussions had started that she was considering the possibility of this working out—that Ranvijay was the one for her. Up until now, she had agonized over worst-case scenarios, assuming he would expect her to be a stay-at-home wife. And she had been planning and plotting about ways and means to get him to break off their engagement. But now that Ranvijay had showed his full support for her academic and career plans, the thought of being actually married to him struck her for the first time.

It had only just dawned on her that, given Ranvijay's support, it was clear that they were going to get married.

Wow, she thought with a good deal of disbelief mixed with a heady excitement, *I am getting married!*

She looked at Ranvijay with a whole new perspective now. He was tall, about 6 feet 1 inches, had the quintessential Rajput brows with big eyes, and well, what a gorgeous face!

It wasn't like she hadn't noticed how good-looking Ranvijay was the first time she saw him, but she hadn't let that distract her from her life's plan. Handsome is what handsome does, she had always believed, and now that Ranvijay had promised her his support so simply and honestly, without any conditions or rules, it made her heart ache. In this moment, she was a mixture of nerves at recognizing that her life was taking a turn right here, and of an unfamiliar shyness at the sudden realization that Ranvijay was going to be her husband.

And it showed on her face.

'Are you okay?' Ranvijay asked.

'Yes, I'm okay,' she had said breathlessly, before gathering her composure and adding, 'and yes, I'm okay with marrying you.'

At this abrupt statement, Ranvijay's eyebrows shot up.

'You asked if I want to marry you,' she explained. 'I do.'

Now, Ranvijay smiled, which made his beautiful eyes twinkle. And this would've remained a sweet, romantic moment, had Meera not remembered an important addendum.

'Oh, one last thing,' she said with a straight face, 'I hope you, or your parents, will not demand a baby soon after we get married?'

Choking on his coffee at this direct question, Ranvijay shook his head in a no.

He had liked Meera from their very first meeting. She was smart, well-spoken and stunning to look at. But thanks to this coffee meeting, he had now discovered that she was also brave, strong and feisty. Ranvijay knew in that moment how much he admired Meera, and he looked forward to their life together.

'Cool,' said Meera, looking both satisfied and exhausted at once. This conversation had been a mammoth task, after all.

'Cool,' Ranvijay seconded her sentiments. Then, he reached across the table and let his hand rest next to Meera's, palm upwards. Meera looked him in the eye. He looked so open and honest that it made Meera glance away quickly, an unfamiliar warmth filling her heart. Slowly, she reached out her own hand and clasped his. Ranvijay's long fingers curled around her hand in response, holding it almost reverentially.

This gesture was so intimate to them that they said nothing further and simply sat with their hands linked for a few long minutes at the busy coffee shop.

They finished their coffee, still holding hands across the table, and when they were ready to leave, Meera looked at Ranvijay and smiled.

'We'll be fine,' she assured him.

Ranvijay nodded with a smile so bright that Meera felt it lit up their corner of the world.

9

Meera and Ranvijay's wedding was a lavish ceremony with the entire Rajput clan in the region coming together to celebrate the union. The sangeet was a Bollywood treat, and while Meera was not comfortable dancing solo to some cheesy number, Ranvijay enthusiastically danced to a choreographed medley that began with *'Pehli Baar'* from *Dil Dhadakne Do* and ended with Salman Khan's *'Tenu Leke'*.

Although Meera had had several telephone conversations with Vikram Rana before this, when she had called to ask about Ranvijay's whereabouts during his missions, the sangeet festivities was the very first time that Meera actually met Vikram Rana in person. It was clear to her that Ranvijay and Vikram Rana shared a really good rapport and held each other in great affection, almost like real brothers; and she was delighted to find that she instantly felt like part of their equation and could join in on their light-hearted banter.

Although a Rajput, Vikram Rana hadn't lived in Rajasthan and had grown up in the much more cosmopolitan and modern township of Pune, and traditional stuff like some of Meera and Ranvijay's older relatives wearing the *ghoonghat* and using a *hukka* were novelties to him. Ranvijay couldn't help laughing at Rana sir's amazement and good-naturedly pulled his leg about his shocked incredulity at some of the typical Rajput traditions at the wedding.

'We'll educate you on your own culture, sir,' Ranvijay had cheekily offered. Meera had nodded enthusiastically.

'You're under our wing now, Bhai-sa,' Meera had chipped in. 'We'll teach you to be a proper Rajput.'

Rana had laughingly agreed.

According to Meera's friends, it was considered good luck for the bride to sneak a peek at the *baraat* as they arrived. So, Meera did exactly that, hidden behind the curtains of a room on the top floor of the hotel into which they had been booked for the wedding.

The baraat arrived at the venue right on time. She was well impressed at his equestrian skill—perched on a horse for the entire duration, looking as comfortable as he would be were he on a plush recliner in the living room. Around him, Capt. Rana and all his friends danced to a mix of traditional Rajasthani and Bollywood songs.

At the reception, an army band, smartly dressed in their official uniforms, played melodious and mesmerizing music. It added an elegant touch to their wedding.

Before meeting Ranvijay, Meera had very little connection to the Indian Army. Sure she had relatives in the army, from both her mom's and dad's sides of the family, but she'd had no real exposure to the army culture up until now. Meeting Ranvijay had opened a whole new portal for her, giving her a tantalizing glimpse of the life and ways of defence families. And she was in awe!

They had met a few times after their initial rendezvous instigated by Meera. Ranvijay started taking short leaves, three days at the most, and they would meet at their favourite café in Bikaner. Meera knew she was falling in love, and if his shy smile and warm eyes were any indication, she knew that he, too, was falling in love with her. Meera often felt that this was her perfect happily ever after.

They were in Ranvijay's house now, an ancient edifice like her own home, but much more lavish. It was a *haveli*, passed down through generations but well maintained and with modern upgrades.

They finished yet another round of ceremonies—cute, couple games and fun traditions for the new bride, as a way to break the ice with her new family. She was at the dresser, getting ready for dinner, which was going to be a big family affair with the relatives who had come to attend the wedding, as most of them would leave the following morning to make their return journeys back to their homes. Ranvijay was leaning against the balcony door in their room, watching her. The balcony overlooked the stone fountain in the middle of the haveli's manicured garden. Meera had fallen in love with their room and its pretty balcony the moment she stepped into it.

'This can be your study area,' Ranvijay indicated the sheltered nook in the balcony. 'We'll set up a desk here.'

'No. I prefer to sit on the floor and study; I only need a floor cushion or a rug,' Meera shook her head.

'In that case, I'll get you one, pronto!' he saluted, making Meera laugh.

They'd had so many discussions over the past few months—ranging from Meera's engineering-semester schedules to Ranvijay's lack of any fixed schedule as a

Para SF commando. Meera was learning about fauji terms that she had only ever heard in the movies and TV shows—patrol party, anti-terrorism operation, debriefing, mobilization, and so on. It was an eye-opener for Meera that these things actually existed in real life.

'Are army wives allowed to sit on the floor?' she asked. Ranvijay had been giving her pointers to the army wife's life. She felt that there were way too many rules for army wives—and as a born rebel, she wasn't very good at toeing the line.

'It isn't a punishment, my love!' Ranvijay chuckled. 'You can do anything you want. Who can stop you when you set your mind to do something, anyway?' he strolled over to the bed.

'But,' she protested as Ranvijay's long arms reached for her, 'it sounds like the army wife's life is all about rules, regulations and etiquette, and then some more about waiting for the husband.'

'See, the way I see it: rules are necessary; they keep things in order and allow us to focus on the bigger things that matter. Etiquette won't be an issue for you because we've grown up in Rajput families which have instilled manners and decorum into us,' Ranvijay hugged her and rolled over with her until they were both lying side by side on the bed.

'And what about the waiting part?' Meera asked breathlessly, looking at their clasped hands, their fingers intertwined. Ever since their fateful first meeting at the coffee house, they had fallen into a mutually, albeit non-verbally, agreed habit of holding hands whenever possible. She loved the way Ranvijay instinctively reached for her hand to envelop it in his warm grasp. She had never imagined that holding hands could be such an intimate gesture.

'She who waits, also serves,' declared Ranvijay, caressing her hand with his thumb. 'But you don't have to sit around, waiting for me, Meera,' he added, 'you're going to complete your BTech next year, and then we'll figure out things as we go along.'

'We will,' Meera nodded. She trusted Ranvijay implicitly and knew that together they could work everything out. They had a plan! Meera would join Infosys, go to Mysore for six months or so for her training, while Ranvijay drew close to completing his field-posting tenure. She would then get a transfer to the Infosys Pune campus where Ranvijay would join her, through a peace posting either in Pune or in a nearby area.

Just so Meera wouldn't feel disappointed later on, Ranvijay had made it abundantly clear, right at the beginning, that his postings were not in his hands as such, and therefore a posting in Pune was a really small possibility.

But what was Meera if not a stubborn and compulsive planner?

After some research, she had discovered that Ranvijay had a strong chance at getting posted to one of the various Indian Army training centres as an instructor—near the city of Indore would be the most convenient for her, as Infosys had a massive campus in Indore. If not, she could always change jobs and try to get into TCS instead, another tech giant with a big campus in Indore.

Ranvijay drew her closer. 'Now let's figure out how much time we have to ourselves before dinner.' He kissed her forehead tenderly and Meera felt a frisson of delight race down her spine. As Ranvijay's lips found hers, she sent a silent prayer to the heavens, thanking God for his existence.

An hour later, she was all dressed, looking gorgeous in an orange chiffon Rajputi poshak with a *zari* border. Ranvijay wore a kurta paired with jeans. They walked down together to the al fresco dinner party in their front lawn, looking like royalty.

Meera couldn't stop smiling. This really was her happily ever after.

* * *

'Is this true?' Meera asked Ranvijay. They were in their room in the late afternoon, in a tangle of arms and legs, skin against skin, watching a news channel. The anchor on the screen was debating the disturbing rise of Pakistan-sponsored terror activities in Kashmir with a bunch of panellists, one of whom had just declared that the two countries were inevitably inching towards a full-blown war.

'Could there really be a war?'

'This is mere conjecture,' Ranvijay said, stroking her arm, tracing tiny, delicious circles on her skin. Meera tried not to get distracted—again.

'But, seriously, what if it is true? Could you be captured by terrorists or the Pakistani Army?' she asked.

'God, no. It's not true. Neither of the countries wants a war, Meera. The situation in Kashmir is unfortunate but that's what the army is there for—to maintain the peace,' Ranvijay replied. 'And as for getting captured by enemy forces, every Special Forces commando is trained for situations like these. We know exactly what to do in dire conditions when the enemy is getting the upper hand, or if one of us gets captured. And I have my own protocols anyway.' He winked conspiratorially.

'And what are those?' Meera asked.

'Number one is to safeguard my troops. They are my priority. And number two is to kill as many of the bastards as I can before they kill me,' Ranvijay shrugged, his tone light and matter of fact. Meera broke out in goosebumps.

'Please, stop! Stop! Stop!' she begged, turning away from him, her back against his stomach now. 'I'm sorry I asked!'

Ranvijay wrapped his arm around her waist and drew her close. 'Why?' he whispered.

'This is all so dangerous. It scares me to even think that you're going back to this job in a few days!'

'It is dangerous, but someone's got to do it,' said Ranvijay.

'Ranvijay, I'm in no mood for jokes,' she stiffened in his embrace. 'Doesn't it worry you that there could be an actual war, and that you'll have to be in it?' The mere thought of Ranvijay involved in a war terrified her. She didn't even have the courage to turn around and face him when she asked the question foremost in her mind, 'What if something happens to you, Ranvijay?'

Ranvijay's arm tightened around her. After a beat, Ranvijay said, '*Yuddh hee toh veer ka praman hai*, Meera. War is the ultimate proof of a braveheart.'

A chill ran down Meera's spine. She sat up and faced Ranvijay, searching his face for any emotion. There was only an immense peace and calmness on his handsome face.

'That's a line from one of my favourite poems. It has been my favourite for many years now and I live by this verse, Meera,' Ranvijay said, reaching for her hand. He sat up as well. 'To fight a war that you believe in; to be a part of a war that is fought to protect all that you hold dear and sacred; a war in which you fight not for personal gain but for a greater cause is like a holy quest to me. The war is proof that there are those who are willing to overcome the most basic instinct of survival to fight for what they have to protect. I may be against any war that is fought for paltry things like territory or resources or political power, but it'll be my honour, *our* honour, Meera, to contribute to a war that is fought to safeguard our country and its people.'

Meera struggled to find words to reply to his amazing sentiment. She hugged him tight and he embraced her back. Meera repeated the line several times in her mind.

Yuddh hee toh veer ka praman hai.

She silently prayed that it would never come to that.

10

It was almost twenty days after the wedding, and it was time for Ranvijay to return to duty.

'My life feels like a Disney movie,' Meera said to Ranvijay, who was inspecting his suitcase before closing it for the final time. Meera had been thinking about this new life. Ranvijay was going back to his work after their wedding, leaving her in her new home with his parents. She felt like a fairytale princess, destined for the happily ever after, but had hit her first glitch in her story. She knew she would eventually get her perfectly planned happy ending; she just had to deal with some minor hiccups in the meanwhile.

But *meanwhile* was the hardest. Watching Ranvijay pack his stuff from around their room was making her sad beyond belief. She thought she had it all under control with all her plans and schedules in place, and yet here she was. On the verge of crying.

'Which one? *Beauty and the Beast*?' Ranvijay joked.

'Ha, ha, ha,' Meera mock laughed and rolled her eyes. 'Actually, *Beauty and the Beast* was good. All Disney movies are good.' After a second, she added thoughtfully, 'As long as our story is not Ariel's, I'm good.'

'Why? What's wrong with the singing mermaid?' Ranvijay clearly hadn't watched the full movie.

'Well, she forfeits her voice to be with her prince, but then he leaves her,' Meera shrugged. 'She probably dies soon after.'

Ranvijay sat behind her on the edge of the bed and put his arms around her. Resting his chin on her shoulder, he said, 'You know I'm not abandoning you, right?'

'No, yeah. I know,' she said, her voice low and shaky.

'Meera, my love,' Ranvijay turned her around, 'don't be sad. This is temporary; just as we discussed, remember? You finish your degree, I'll finish my tenure and we'll keep meeting every few months! And when we're both done, we'll plan the next steps and conquer that goal as well.'

Meera nodded, not trusting her voice.

'We are warriors, Meera,' Ranvijay said, kissing her forehead. 'And you are my *veer yoddha*, my warrior-princess.'

'Easy for you to say, you're a brave fauji. Maybe I'm not all that brave.'

'You are; I saw it in your eyes the first time I met you, Meera. There's a fire in your belly that keeps you on track to follow your goal. It's a fire that fuels courage, instils bravery.'

'Not as brave as you are, going back to the terrorism-infested area with that big smile on your face,' Meera muttered, 'don't think I haven't noticed it.'

'My heart is distraught at the thought of leaving without you, Meera, and you know this.'

Slowly, Meera nodded. She knew.

'But where I'm going is my karmbhoomi. And that is a place for the brave and the driven, Meera. It isn't a place for cowards. You know that just as you are dedicated to your goal, I'm dedicated to my duty. It drives me.'

'I know. And while I like that balance between us, I just wish that your duty and my goal could've been better aligned, so we could tread this path together.'

'So, what you're saying is that you'll miss me, right?' Ranvijay chuckled and hugged her tight.

'What I'm saying is that I'll kill you if you're not back here in time on your leaves, as you promised.'

'Your wish is my command, ma'am.'

They laughed and held on to each other for as long as they could. Eventually Ranvijay had to say goodbye, leaving Meera in tears.

* * *

Meera was in the sixth semester of BTech. Her college had recently offered an additional certification course on ethical hacking which she had spontaneously taken up and was thoroughly enjoying. She had always been a bright student, and her special interest was in codes and computers, so she was making the most of this opportunity to study an advanced subject like hacking.

Every day, Meera would have breakfast with Ranvijay's parents, whom she had begun to love like her own. Ranvijay's father was the life of every party and gathering, a suave man with a thick moustache and a smiling face. His mom was graceful and soft in conduct, but assertive nonetheless. Ranvijay was an only son, and his parents loved having Meera around to pamper and take care of. After breakfast, Ranvijay's dad would drop off Meera to her college, before he headed to his own work. She would return home by 4.30 p.m. and have tea with her mother-in-law.

This was the time when she would hear stories about Ranvijay's childhood, his early days at the National Defence Academy and his friends. Later, both of them would prepare dinner and when her father-in-law returned home, they would all sit together, chat and eat. Very often, when it wasn't too hot or too cold, Meera would go on long post-dinner walks with her mother-in-law, chatting about everything under the sun. Meera loved the ease with which her new life had fallen into place.

'Ranvijay's mom made me daal baati last week, when I said I was missing your food, Ma,' Meera told her mom, during one of her frequent visits to her parent's home. Being in the same city, she got to see them often, 'even though neither of them eats daal baati because of their high cholesterol; she only makes it for Ranvijay whenever he's home on *chutti*. And now for me.'

Ma smiled. She had heard so much about Ranvijay and his family from Meera and seeing how well her daughter had found her place not just in her new home but also in the hearts of her new family, was something she was very proud of. And also relieved. She knew that with a girl as strong-headed as her youngest, relationships could have gone either way.

So, she said a little prayer to thank Bajrang Bali, and affectionately added some more ghee to the halwa she was cooking for Meera.

* * *

Ranvijay and Meera stepped out of the café, hand in hand. Ranvijay was on leave and Meera was on cloud nine. Ranvijay was so warm, kind and caring, that sometimes her heart ached for no reason at all. She squeezed his hand and smiled up at him. As usual, Ranvijay was in his version of civvies, a tucked-in, collared tee-shirt and basic blue jeans, with a leather belt. Meera always pointed out that only faujis dressed like this, and Ranvijay would shrug, smiling. I can't do distressed jeans or sloppy tee-shirts, he would say. Meera liked to tease him, but she secretly loved this about Ranvijay—his confidence and his refusal to fit in. She was the same; they were like peas in a pod.

She was ecstatic today. Not only was Ranvijay here for two whole weeks, but she had just received a commendation in the ethical hacking course she had taken. This had made her so happy. Code spoke to her, and her mind was inherently analytical, which made her an excellent hacker. She could connect unrelated pieces of code and information and analyse the combined information to deduce a brand-new solution. She had shared every little detail about her progress with Ranvijay and he was so proud of her that it made Meera's happiness grow tenfold.

'I am so proud of you, Meera,' he had said multiple times.

'I love making you proud,' Meera answered. 'Just knowing that you're rooting for me gives me fuel.'

'Fuel for your fire,' Ranvijay said, smiling.

'May it always burn bright.'

'Amen,' said Ranvijay and hugged Meera.

* * *

The two weeks flew by in a jiffy, and then it was time for Ranvijay to leave.

He had to return to Kashmir, the location where his Para SF unit was currently based, to rejoin duty. Being married to an army officer, she knew, of course, that his duty took precedence before anyone, even herself. For a soldier, the country is his or her first priority, everyone else came after that. On most days, Meera was proud of this . . . but not today. Today she was a mess. She didn't want to let him go.

'I'm going to miss you,' she told him, tears in her eyes. 'Will you miss me?'

'I'll miss you more than you know,' he said in a solemn voice. 'Kashmir is heaven on earth, Meera. There is poetry and romance everywhere I look. Being there without you is unbearable.' Meera hugged him tight. 'But I'll be back before you know it! You keep working hard to finish at the top of your batch and meanwhile, I'll give a hard time to the bastards who try to cross the border from the other side.' He winked.

'One, I'm already top of my batch,' replied Meera sullenly, 'and two, don't you dare bring up terrorists with me. I already get nightmares.'

At this, Ranvijay laughed heartily.

That night, Meera had terrible nightmares. She woke up exhausted, and it was time for Ranvijay to go. That was the fauji life, after all.

In the morning, just as Ranvijay was about to leave after breakfast, Meera felt a fresh pang of sadness in her heart. She didn't want to live like this, from chutti to chutti.

'Where's my medal?' she asked as he tied his shoelaces.

'Um, what?'

'My medal for serving without a salary?' Meera clarified.

'Meera . . .' he said with a small smile, at once understanding where she was going with this.

'You said, "She who waits also serves." So, I'm serving the army, the country. But without a salary. So, Capt. Ranvijay Chauhan, I deserve a medal at the very least, don't you think?'

Ranvijay laughed and drew her into his arms. Meera invariably grew edgy, sad, jittery and anxious every time he had to leave, and her coping mechanism was anger. He found it adorable when she sulked like this.

Leaving her was tough on Ranvijay too. But he didn't dwell on it. This was a way of life for him, and it was one for which he had worked hard. He had studied hard to get through the NDA and then toiled to get into Para SF. While a piece of his heart was always with Meera, he also knew that duty would always trump his personal desires.

And so, he smiled and started to make Meera laugh as he always did. He drew her close and kissed her passionately making her gasp and giggle. And then, he kissed her forehead and left. Meera's forehead felt like it had been branded by a red-hot iron where his lips had touched her skin. It was like this every time he kissed her before leaving. She cherished the lingering touch of his lips long after Ranvijay had left for duty, and sometimes she wished his touch would leave a mark, so that she would have a memento to cherish.

* * *

'It was okay,' Meera said, pressing the phone to her ear. The network wasn't very strong where Ranvijay was, and she could hear the static more than Ranvijay's voice. 'I could've done better.'

'Getting two questions wrong in your final paper isn't bad, Meera,' Ranvijay said, and she could sense his smile. 'Live a little, celebrate it! Your degree is completed!'

'I'll "live a little" when the degree finally arrives. Or at least when the results do,' said Meera. 'For now, I'm trying to forget this last exam and focus on my packing for Mysore. Hopefully, that'll distract me.'

Meera was being paranoid. She had been able to nail all her subjects in the final exams of her BTech degree, but she strived for perfection each time—it could get exhausting for most people, but not for her. Moreover, adding to her woes was the fact that Ranvijay's leave was cancelled at the last minute because of some urgent mission. So now she had to go alone to Mysore, and although she knew she could handle it—Infosys was managing everything for new joiners anyway—she was sad at not having a few days of peace and quiet with Ranvijay in a city that was brand new to her, before she started her training programme.

The silver lining was the fact that she was indeed going to Mysore to join Infosys as per her long-standing plans. The company had selected Meera during a campus placement drive in her engineering college in Bikaner, and she was going to join duty the following week. Her parents, naturally, were not in favour, especially her father. He was uncomfortable about her going alone to a strange city, and he was appalled that her husband and her in-laws were letting this happen.

Her in-laws weren't too sure either—they didn't want Meera to go because it felt unsafe for her to be alone in a new city. But Ranvijay supported the decision, and they didn't want to interfere. They would've preferred Meera stayed with them until Ranvijay was posted to an area that was termed 'peace posting', after which they were sure that Meera and Ranvijay could live a normal life and perhaps have kids. Both sets of parents had now started to drop subtle hints about wanting to have grandchildren, much to Meera's exasperation and Ranvijay's delight at her adorable irritation.

But Ranvijay had handled everyone and everything, even from a remote location. It often amazed Meera how beautifully Ranvijay was able to manage family dynamics without losing his calm. So now, thanks to his management skills and his negotiation skills with their parents, Meera was going to get on a train to Mysore in a few days.

'People talk such nonsense, my child,' Ranvijay's mom said to Meera one day.

To which Meera had replied, 'Mumma, people will always say something or the other. Should one give up on their life and stop chasing their dreams because of what people say?'

Almost as if on cue, Ranvijay had video-called just then. He handled the rest, addressed all concerns and promised Meera's wellbeing to his concerned mother.

'Your daughter-in-law is a warrior-princess, Mom. And you chose her for me. You know that the fire she holds in her belly is the same fire that I have in mine. She can handle everything as long as we're on her side. And especially you—you need to be in her corner. You need to support her because I am not there and the dads on both sides can be pretty tough. She needs the strength that you have to keep her going.'

Ranvijay's mother nodded, thinking back on each time and every moment when her heart felt like it was shattering into a million pieces because her only child, Ranvijay, was in a profession where duty came before his own life. She had first experienced this twinge of dismay when a much younger Ranvijay was going to join the academy after clearing the NDA exam. It felt dangerous and scary, and she had assumed the worst, like every mother who sent off her precious child to join the army. And then she experienced it every time he would tell them that he was off on a mission. He didn't tell them often, for obvious reasons, besides the secrecy he had pledged; he never wanted them to worry about him while all he was doing was his duty. But a mother's heart knew. Ranvijay's mom once read somewhere that fearlessness was the first requisite of spirituality, that cowards can never be moral. And she knew in her heart that her son, her brave, kind, thoughtful son, fit this description well. It engendered both fear and pride in her.

She held herself with a strength she could draw upon in moments like these—the famous Rajput courage which had inspired numerous folktales and songs, the bravery she drew from knowing that her personal sacrifice was for a noble cause.

She promised Ranvijay that she would not only support, but also encourage and guide Meera to the best of her capacity.

11

In Mysore, the Infosys campus never failed to impress Meera. It was sprawling, grand and so well managed. The fact that she was finding her training modules exciting was a bonus.

After a few months of rigorous training there, Meera received the news that she was being sent to the Pune campus—almost as if by a stroke of luck. Her prayers were being answered, and Ranvijay sent her a big bunch of flowers with a note that said: '*Congratulations on dreams coming true—this is just the start, my warrior-princess.*'

The day of the move from Mysore to Pune came quickly, and Ranvijay called Meera. He couldn't come down to help her move cities yet again, and he was devastated. But this time, there was some good news—Capt. Rana was on his annual leave and was going to be in Pune.

'Rana sir will meet you at the station, don't forget,' Ranvijay said to her on the phone. 'I know you don't want any assistance and can manage things on your own but let me do this much for my own satisfaction. I can't be there with you at this time, and it's killing me. I'll be at peace knowing that you had reliable help and support during your first time in an entirely new city. So just humour me, please.'

'Rana bhai-sa is like family, Ranvijay. And every time I've called him, frantic and worried sick about not being able to contact you, when you're off for missions in some godforsaken place without a phone or a network for days, he has been helpful and kind to me—of course, I'll be nice to him, have a little faith in me!' Meera exclaimed, laughing now. She knew Ranvijay was partly worried that she would try to set up her life in Pune all by herself and not want any help—he sometimes called it her Rajputi woman pride, about which there are multiple tales in our history. But he wanted to make things as easy and comfortable for her, as he could, even if remotely. And he believed that Capt. Rana would be able to help Meera a lot, since he was a Puneri and knew the city well.

'I mean, I don't *need* help and support, I can manage things. Infosys is providing pick-up and everything anyway, but I'll be on my best behaviour, and it'll be nice to meet him and get some gossip about you anyway,' she added.

Capt. Rana had been of massive help to her whenever Ranvijay was out on various operations with no way for her to contact him. She and Ranvijay usually talked a lot over the phone, thanks to mobile networks everywhere, even in the valley, but there were times when he was out of touch for long periods of time without any contact.

The longest till date had been three days.

Three days of unadulterated misery for Meera.

Ranvijay, however, unfailingly called to inform her in advance of any possible radio silence from his end, hoping that she wouldn't worry too much. But worry and fear of the what-ifs often outweighed logic for all army family members, and at such times, Capt. Vikram Rana was Meera's lifeline to sanity. She called him and he calmed her down by telling her when Ranvijay would be able to call her back, or at least relaying non-classified information so she knew that Ranvijay was safe. That was all she wanted more than anything in those terrifying moments of worry, and she was grateful for that.

* * *

By the end of December 2013, Meera felt more or less settled in Pune, a city that had featured prominently in her plans. After the initial training at Infosys, she was assigned to a special wing that worked in defence research, unlike most engineering graduates who often started in IT departments. This was a time when the Indian defence sector was booming. The Indian government had made the importance of new defence equipment—such as drones, anti-drone systems, missiles, air-defence systems—quite clear in the recent past and had focused on the localization of production of reliable defence equipment and their critical components. This, in turn, had resulted in large and sustainable opportunities for domestic players, and Infosys, as one of the leaders in Aerospace and defence consulting in India, was working in other areas of defence technology as well, including high-tech intelligence systems which included AI and advanced equipment. However, this was still in a nascent stage, but Meera was elated to be assigned to the project because of the promise it held.

Capt. Rana had been an excellent support to Meera in the first week of her arriving in Pune. By the end of the week, Meera not only knew the best food joints in her area, but had also met Capt. Rana's parents, who were warm, welcoming and had volunteered to be her local guardians, and his girlfriend, Sameera, who was an entertainment lawyer in Mumbai and was as loving as she was stunning. Meera and Sameera instantly added each other on social media, just as Capt. Rana's mother tagged both of them in an Instagram post captioned 'My heart is full'—it was a picture of all five of them around a table laden with food.

A new phase was starting for Meera, and she couldn't wait to ace it. She knew that the following year, between July and August of 2014, Ranvijay would be posted out of Kashmir, and she was ready to knuckle down and do her best at this job in the meanwhile, so that she could get a hybrid working arrangement from quarter three of 2014, or a favourable campus transfer according to Ranvijay's next posting.

Everything was working out. Her job was exciting. She was loving her life in this new city that bustled with students and first-time jobbers, and a young population that added to its overall, high-decibel energy.

It's all going to plan, Meera thought. She touched a wooden table and kissed her fingers to be safe from *buri nazar* because both, the present and the future looked bright.

Then came the news about Jammu.

Ranvijay called one morning and, in a voice that sounded normal on the surface but betrayed his disappointment underpinning it, he told Meera that he was being posted to Jammu for a few months. Why was this move planned so suddenly? For how long was he going to be stationed in Jammu? He could provide no answers to her and she sensed his deep dejection. Ranvijay was a master at disguising his emotions, especially the ones he thought would worry or trouble Meera and their families. And he hid it well this time around as well. But Meera was sure she could detect the undercurrent of sadness in his voice, even if she decided to let it go for now, because whatever the cause, a chance to live with her husband was not something that an army wife willingly forgoes. There would be plenty of time to cross-examine him later, she thought.

Meera spoke with her manager at work, and was granted permission to work remotely for a month, from Jammu. All she needed was her company laptop, a secure VPN and a steady Internet connection.

Meera felt excited and full of joy at the prospect of spending time with her husband. Although Ranvijay had no idea about the duration of his Jammu attachment, she knew she could get an extension on her remote-working arrangement if required. She packed a month's supply of clothes and other necessities and set off for Jammu airport within a week of receiving the news. Some unexpected peace-posting time with Ranvijay was the best thing she could have asked for, even if it was for a short duration. Meera silently thanked God for her luck which had turned ever since she met Ranvijay. *If humans can be each other's lucky charm, he is definitely mine*, she thought, as she sat down in her window seat on the plane to Jammu. Ranvijay was going to pick her up at the airport, and she was excited to meet him, to be with him at his workplace and live a semblance of a normal-married-couple life for the time being. She was so happy she couldn't stop smiling.

In Jammu, as she emerged through the airport gates, Meera realized that she was almost lightheaded with excitement at the prospect of seeing Ranvijay after these long months. She decided she was going to run into his arms the moment she saw him and wasn't going to let go for a long, long time.

Smiling in anticipation, she looked around, trying to spot him. And then she did. She saw him walk towards her and froze. Her plans of flinging herself into his arms were summarily shelved. Meera felt rooted to the spot and unable to move. In fact, she couldn't even take her eyes off him.

From the maroon beret on his head to the combat uniform on his body, from the tan on his handsome face to the gold-rimmed RayBan aviators on his eyes—Ranvijay looked like some sort of a warrior God walking the earth after his victory.

A thrill of surprise and delight ran through her, as Meera realized that this was the first time she was actually seeing Ranvijay in his uniform. *What a sight!* she thought to herself, as she stood watching him walk towards her, taking in every detail of her handsome paratrooper husband in all his combat-uniformed glory.

'Hey, you!' Ranvijay said with a big smile as he got closer, and hugged Meera tightly.

'Hey,' Meera managed.

'What?'

'Nothing . . . just, all this is . . . wow!' Meera said, indicating all of him with both her hands. 'I mean, you could've at least warned a girl before unleashing all this hotness. I could've had a heart attack, you know.'

'Well,' Ranvijay winked, 'mission accomplished.' Both of them laughed and hugged each other again.

On the way to the Jammu cantonment, Ranvijay kept talking and Meera kept quiet, taking him in in his environment. This was her Ranvijay, but in a new light, and she loved it. Meera knew the significance of the maroon beret, Ranvijay had explained it to her during one of their covert meetings before they got married. The maroon beret was reserved for the most distinguished and elite commandoes across all the armies of the world. And in the Indian Army, it was reserved for the paratroopers by virtue of their tough selection, rigorous training and continuous deployment and preparation. She knew this! However, seeing him in one was a completely different thing than knowing about it in theory. Her heart swelled with pride as she looked at Ranvijay.

In Jammu, time flew. With Ranvijay holding a desk job for the first time since they got married, Meera and Ranvijay lived like any regular couple and enjoyed little moments of togetherness which were otherwise a luxury for them. They ate together, went on long walks every day within the cantonment and on long drives on the NH-1 Alpha almost every weekend. They went out into the city to try out the various cafés and restaurants. And most importantly, they spent every possible minute together. Meera loved this life! She knew she would enjoy Ranvijay's peace posting when it happened, and now she eagerly looked forward to it more than before.

'This Jammu plan is the best thing to have happened, seriously,' she had told Ranvijay one evening, during their walk in the green and serene cantonment grounds.

'Wasn't a part of your plan, though,' Ranvijay had teased her.

'As long as you're with me, it's okay to deviate from the plan a bit, I guess,' she had laughed.

Little did she know that it would be the last time she would see Ranvijay.

* * *

April 2014

Meera felt dizzy and even before she could process the words or the information, she collapsed on the floor of her parents' veranda. Her mother ran to catch her before she hit her head on the ground, shouting for help.

Meera had come to Bikaner for the first time after moving to Pune. She had taken a week off to meet both their parents and had arrived laden with gifts for everyone, which she had bought with her earnings. Ranvijay was due for a new posting in a couple of months or so, and they had decided that April would be a good time for her to meet family before they moved to yet another place.

Ranvijay's parents were at the station to pick her up, and they had happy tears in their eyes when she stepped off the train to greet them. It must be tough for them, Meera had thought in that moment, having both their son and daughter-in-law away from home. Maybe we will be able to convince them to move in with us when Ranvijay has a peace posting, she decided.

After the tearful welcome, they dropped off Meera at her parents' home. Meera promised to divide her time equally between the two houses. In any case, now that she was in town, both families would get together for plenty of meals. She had planned everything, and it was bound to go perfectly!

But she had been distracted since the previous day. Ranvijay had told her that he was up for another mission and might not be available for around twenty-four to thirty hours. As the day dragged on and she hadn't heard from him, Meera grew restless. She had called Ranvijay's cell phone several times but it had been switched off, as it usually was during a mission. She knew he didn't carry his cell phone when he went on a mission, and the phone would be turned off until he was back at the base. Hours went by, and then she had called Capt. Rana, which was usually her last resort.

Capt. Rana had answered her call and had reassured her that Ranvijay would be back by the next afternoon, and it have given her a modicum of relief. Although the commandoes never mentioned anything specific, she knew that they were always in touch with the party out on a mission, and she was relieved to know that Ranvijay had been in contact with his paltan.

That conversation with Capt. Rana had taken place only the previous evening! And then this phone call from the CO . . . it didn't make any sense . . .

'Ranvijay has made the supreme sacrifice . . .' the CO had said on the phone, in a low and serious voice. And then he paused, as if gathering more courage for this conversation. What did 'supreme sacrifice' mean, Meera wondered, because in that moment, her mind refused to function.

'His body will be sent . . .' the CO started again, but Meera didn't hear anything more. Her body shut down from shock and she fell to the ground unconscious.

When Meera regained consciousness, she felt disoriented. At first, she couldn't remember what had happened. Sitting up in her bed in her parents' house, she looked around. *What time is it?* she wondered. *When did I fall asleep?* she was puzzled.

And then it all came back to her like a storm so powerful that she felt the air escape her lungs. She cried out his name and broke down sobbing, as her parents rushed into her room.

Ranvijay was no more.

* * *

It had been a week since Meera and her family had received the news about Ranvijay, and she still couldn't believe what had happened. Every few hours, she felt like she had forgotten that Ranvijay was dead and would—for a second—look for her phone to call him. She would wake up after dreaming of him, dreams that felt all too real. She would pick her phone up to check if Ranvijay had texted her. And in all these scenarios, her mind would swiftly bring back the memory of the dark wooden coffin in the front lawn of Ranvijay's parental house. And Ranvijay's name written on it in bold white letters.

She hadn't come to terms with Ranvijay not being with her any more, of his being gone forever. To her, it almost felt like when Ranvijay was away on missions and she would worry about not hearing from him, but he would always eventually come back to her. She knew that he was not coming back this time; she knew that this time, it was final.

But knowing something in your head, and feeling it in your heart are two different things.

Meera's heart felt like it was breaking; it felt like the process of her heartbreak was continuously underway with no relief. It just broke and broke and then, broke further. And with every painful stab she felt in her chest, Meera felt weaker. Physically, mentally and emotionally.

Where do I go from here, Ranvijay? she often talked to him in her mind. *What am I supposed to do now?*

No answers came.

Meera had always been a logical person who worked on facts, not fantasy. She had always been level-headed, and always planned her next steps in life carefully. She had a clear vision and no one could deter her from pursuing her goal.

But Meera was an altogether different person now. Her mind that was otherwise logical and clear would just not accept what had happened. She knew Ranvijay was no more, she was there every step of the way in Ranvijay's state-organized last rites, and she was the one to whom the two soldiers had marched up, to hand over the neatly folded Indian flag which had covered Ranvijay's coffin, just before the final ritual.

And yet, there were parts of her that had still not accepted that Ranvijay would never smile at her again, would never hold her hand in his again. A tiny part of her still hoped against all logic that Ranvijay would come back to her. The closed-coffin funeral that Ranvijay received ensured that Meera got no respite from the onslaught of grief. His body had been so badly mutilated that she didn't even get to see his face for one last time.

Why am I being subjected to this ruthlessness? she asked the heavens.

What have I done to deserve this?

What did Ranvijay do to deserve this?

There were no answers, only grief. And her bereavement took over like a dark shroud that refused to lift. She woke up every morning from unsettling dreams and for the first few blissful seconds, she forgot the tragedy that had befallen her. But then she would remember, and her heart would break again. She would weep bitterly just as she had wept the first time upon hearing the sorrowful news. One day, she had to be rushed to a nearby hospital by her in-laws, when she passed out from crying so much.

Grief is just the love you have for the person who isn't here any more, Ranvijay's mother told her one day, stroking Meera's head lovingly and wiping the tears from her own eyes. Meera had moved to her in-laws' house immediately after they received the dreadful news, before Ranvijay's body arrived at the house.

'But what do we do with this love, now that he isn't here any more, Mumma?' she asked.

'I don't know, beta,' her mother-in-law sobbed. 'I just don't know.'

They were all suffering together. And yet, Meera found the state of grieving a lonely one.

Where do I go from here . . . she asked once again, expecting Ranvijay to tell her, guide her, motivate her.

But he remained silent. She was on her own. No plans, no direction.

12

It had been a month since the day Meera answered the fateful call from Ranvijay's CO.

A month since she had received the news that had changed her life.

She was in Bikaner. Infosys had granted her bereavement leave but she wasn't even sure whether she wanted to return to her job to fulfil her goals and her plans beyond this. Everything had changed. Ranvijay's murder has transformed everything. Sometimes Meera wasn't even sure whether she wanted to continue just existing, whether she was even capable of living in this world without Ranvijay. The sheer hopelessness of her life made her want to give up on everything.

How is this fair? she often wondered with rage.

How is he dead, but I'm still alive? the question haunted Meera constantly.

For the first time in her life, Meera didn't have a plan.

She had been told officially that Ranvijay was killed in action during a mission. He was one of four martyrs killed by one of the most feared terrorist commanders in a forest in Kashmir. However, it was from the news media that she learnt that a group of terrorists had tracked and targeted Capt. Ranvijay Chauhan specifically because of his outstanding record in eliminating many jihadis from the valley. According to the journalists, this terrorist group had cunningly orchestrated this entire ruse for weeks to mislead the Indian intelligence.

Of course, every channel told the story in their own way—the details of this incident were certainly classified—but in today's connected world, news travelled fast.

The channels debated the state of Indian intelligence for hours at length, with various panels stacked with veteran army officers, decorated retired generals, defence journalists and anyone with even the slightest authority on the subject.

As images of a young and smiling Ranvijay in his Indian Army uniform and maroon beret dominated the TV screens on loop, it was safe to say that the entire nation was in shock and grieving, not only because of the killing of yet another Indian soldier, but also appalled at the brutal manner in which the assassination had been carried out.

Some channels ran profiles on jihadi terror organizations that they suspected were behind the murder of Capt. Ranvijay; some discussed the failure of the Indian Army's intelligence due to its severe lack of advanced technology; and some played patriotic songs with video footage of Ranvijay's last rites on loop. Meera watched them all. And still, Ranvijay's murder seemed surreal to Meera—like it was happening to someone else. *What is happening?* she would often look around and wonder. *This can't be real.*

Nothing made sense to her.

Condolences received directly from the country's big political leaders.

Prayer meetings held for Ranvijay to which the entire city seemed to have flocked to pay their respects.

Meeting the Chief of Army Staff and his wife, Meera couldn't say a single word and just stood staring at the ground.

Is Ranvijay really gone? Meera often found herself thinking. *But we had a plan.*

The Indian Army assured her that they would do everything in their power to help her. From Ranvijay's veer yoddha, his warrior-princess, she was a Veer Nari now, a war widow.

Because this was a war, wasn't it?

Meera remembered the conversation she'd had with Ranvijay just a few days after their wedding. She remembered being worried after seeing a TV report that said war was imminent between India and Pakistan. But Ranvijay had said that a full-blown war wasn't a possibility. In that moment, Meera had believed him.

But now, she wondered if the meaning of war had changed . . .

In these times, did war still only mean soldiers engaging in hand-to-hand combat, artillery and guns being fired at distant targets and tanks being deployed to destroy the enemy's line of defence?

The truth is that our country is constantly at war, Meera thought. She was sure that what was going on in Kashmir was nothing short of war, even if the governments refused to call it that.

What had happened to Ranvijay was not just a random act of terrorism; it was planned sabotage. This was a premeditated, cold-blooded murder, even if the media didn't have all details. Her family didn't have much more information to go on, so Meera became obsessed with the news.

The same news channels that gave her heart palpitations when Ranvijay was alive, became her solace after his demise. She followed Kashmir-related issues closely. She read articles by defence experts about the turmoil in the area and books by veteran officers who had spent time in the valley. She immersed herself in gaining knowledge about the state of affairs that had cost her husband, the love of her life, his life.

Another thing she because obsessed with was the process of gathering and processing intelligence by the army. She read all she could find about encrypted messages, about informer networks and advanced technology that the West used. She became fixated on the subject because she felt that if the information and intelligence system had been stronger and more reliable, Ranvijay would still be alive.

Ranvijay had been right when he had told her that her mind would be off him only when she was busy studying something. So now, she was studying Kashmir.

* * *

A little more than two months had passed since Ranvijay's demise. Meera continued to stay in the room she had shared with Ranvijay at his parents' house ever since her husband's death, except for the week when she had travelled to Pune to pack up her stuff before returning to Bikaner for good.

Infosys had provided her a remote-working opportunity for the entire year, and she was thankful for that. But work was the last thing on her mind. Meera was still at the lowest ebb she had ever been, both emotionally and mentally.

When will this get back to normal? she wondered. *Will I ever wake up knowing that he is not here any more?* At least that way she wouldn't have to endure the brutal blow she got every morning when the realization hit her.

What a tough life, Meera often thought. *Where do I go from here?*

In her darkest moments, Meera found herself turning to Ranvijay, the way she would sometimes turn to heaven for strength and prayers before his passing. Now, he became the higher power from where she sought strength and to whom she even offered prayers. She would speak to Ranvijay in her mind and heart, and although there were no answers, she found the process comforting.

Why am I still alive and he is dead? His life meant so much more than mine. Meera often debated this in her head. She felt guilty about being the one who was still living and breathing. She knew this was survivor's guilt and a common condition for people who went through traumatic incidents. But this knowledge did nothing to help.

She was sitting cross-legged in the balcony of their room while she sobbed silently—a skill she had developed over the past few months so that no one could hear her breaking down, yet again. She had grown up being the strong one in the house, and her current state felt like a let-down, even to herself. But she couldn't help it, she felt gloomy and unworthy all the time.

'I'm not the person you thought I was, Ranvijay,' she said, silently. 'I am no warrior-princess. I'm a coward, ready to give up. And I don't know how to stop.'

'Just the bare minimum of living, just the minimal act of being alive when you're not, feels like a war to me, Ranvijay,' she said to him, in her mind, 'and I'm not made for wars.'

And just then, for the first time since he had passed away, Meera felt like Ranvijay's voice was reaching out to her from the depths of her own heart. His voice! It was so real that she could almost hear him whisper it in her ears, goosebumps appeared on her neck: '*Yuddh hee toh veer ka praman hai* (the courage to fight a war that you believe in is the proof of a warrior).'

A warrior is a person who conjures up God-like courage to give his all for something bigger than himself.

Or herself, she corrected.

She was Ranvijay's warrior-princess, after all. And not all wars looked alike, she realized in that moment. There are some wars that one has to fight on one's own.

After months and months of a period so dark that the world had started to look grey around her, Meera smiled. In the balcony, where Ranvijay had set up a study desk for her just days after they got married, Meera finally found her war to conquer.

It was there that Meera decided to build herself into the yoddha, the fierce warrior Ranvijay saw in her.

Her eyes shone with a new resolve, and she held her head high after a season of sorrow. The next steps of her life came to her with extreme clarity, in a flash, like it had been meticulously planned all along in another dimension.

What she wanted to do, where she wanted to go from here was now so clear to her that she did not even flinch at how farfetched it all sounded. She just knew she would do it. It was as though she had been handed a new purpose in life— one that fuelled the fire in her belly that only Ranvijay had recognized.

With new conviction in her eyes, Meera wound her hair into a bun and got up. She paused to glance at the lawn below the balcony, and visions of the coffin containing Ranvijay's body parts being carried in flashed before her eyes, as always.

'I'm going to take the path you chose, Ranvijay,' Meera promised herself. 'I'm going to carry your dreams forward, follow your legacy. That is the only way my life will make sense. This is the only purpose bigger than my grief that can keep me going,' Meera said to the vision of Ranvijay in her mind.

She walked into her room and began researching the next step right away.

13

Meera spent all her free time researching the steps she needed to take to achieve her new goal. She had not shared her plans with anyone in her family yet, because she knew what they would say, how they would react to it. *They would never understand, not one of them*, thought Meera. Her family, although loving and supportive of her to a fault, more so now after Ranvijay's death, were still simple, traditional people who would choose a 'settled' and safe life for her rather than anything unconventional. And Meera wanted nothing to do with their version of being 'settled'. She wanted more—much more.

So, for almost a month, she kept going on her own. She researched every aspect, she planned every step and as soon as she was convinced that she was in a place where she could confidently pull it off, she decided to share the news with her family. She was contemplating inviting her parents over one evening, having both sets of parents sit together for tea, and then telling them what her plan was. She knew none of the four were going to be okay with what she had chosen to do, but it was time that she told them.

And with this, it struck Meera that she was back to handling conflict against her decisions alone, without the support of anyone. Ranvijay had always supported her and had handled family resistance on her behalf. With time, Meera's automatic assumption that there would be opposition to her opinion had faded away. *How liberating it had been to be met with encouragement, to not be plagued by fear of not being accepted*, she thought, as she steeled herself to fight for herself yet again.

The next week, Meera invited her parents over. She sat them down along with Ranvijay's parents in the living room and told them she had an important announcement to make. All four of them had come together over the past few months to take care of Meera, who had been lost and dejected for most of this time. They had provided support and unconditional love to Meera in the best way they could. While open communication wasn't the strong suit in either of the dads, the mothers had taken it upon themselves to help Meera get back to some sort of normalcy. They had talked to Meera, showered her with love and care and had coaxed her to share the burden of her sorrow. But Meera was on a different plane altogether. On the outside, she remained the stalwart who wouldn't dream of revealing the pain of her heartache which she knew would only devastate her family—choosing instead to keep a stiff upper lip, to deal with her emotions and her internal turmoil herself and to chart out her path alone. Now, she was ready to share her decision with them.

Both sets of parents were simple folks, belonging to an entirely different generation with low awareness about mental health and to them, it looked like Meera was slowly descending into madness. Although, they had noticed a positive change in her over the past few weeks—something which they couldn't really put their finger on, since Meera was not one to wear her heart on her sleeve, but something that had been enough to keep her occupied and busy like she used to be when Ranvijay was alive—a girl on a mission, always up to something bigger, something more challenging. They didn't know whether it was a good sign or not, yet.

In the living room, the normal pleasantries were exchanged and as soon as tea was served, Meera cleared her throat and got ready to speak. Everyone fell silent.

'I don't want to continue living like this,' she began without preamble, looking at each of them by turn. 'I want to create a new life for myself, a life that has a larger purpose.'

'I agree,' said Ranvijay's mom at once. 'And I know what we need to do. We should consider remarriage,' she declared.

Meera's jaw fell open in shock. She'd had no idea her mother-in-law was planning an announcement of her own. Dumbfounded by this outrageous suggestion, Meera looked at her dad. She could see his patent shock and disapproval.

Meera knew her parents and their belief systems well. They were more traditional than Ranvijay's parents in a lot of ways—remarriage was not a common thing in their community and circle, and certainly not something that was seen in the right light. *What will people say?*—Meera was sure her dad was thinking. She then stole a look at her mother. She sat there, the end of the dupatta of her poshak covering her head as always, an unreadable expression on her face.

Ranvijay's father looked shocked as well. *Enough*, thought Meera. She needed to nip this ridiculous discussion in the bud by telling them her plan, but her father beat her to it.

'This can never happen!' Meera's father declared in a loud voice. 'Meera is a widow now; and in our family, widows don't remarry!'

'What kind of regressive traditions are you talking about, bhaisahab?' Ranvijay's mom countered. 'If she's a widow now, should she be expected to remain one all her life? She's only twenty-three years old!'

'It's her destiny,' replied Meera's father.

'It isn't right to force her to live the life of a widow. Our son would never want her to be unhappy,' Ranvijay's mom pleaded to the room.

But Meera had had enough. From her seat, she addressed the room in an eerily calm voice: 'I will not remarry.'

The room went quiet once again.

'Not now. Not in a year. Not ever,' Meera continued. 'I will not remarry.'

'I told you!' said Meera's father. 'My daughter isn't going to bring shame to my family,' he looked strangely relieved.

'My decision has nothing to do with your values or the family's honour, Papa,' Meera addressed him. 'But I will not marry again.'

She paused and took a deep breath before sharing what she had planned for her future. She braced herself for impact because she knew her announcement wouldn't go down well; but she was prepared to do it alone. While it was her duty to tell them of her decision, she wasn't going to be dependent on their approval.

Before starting, she looked around the room, taking it all in.

It was interesting to note how a family changes through the experiences and challenges they face together. Harrowing in this case, and yet, spellbinding.

As much as Ranvijay's mother's courage and love touched her, she didn't want to remarry. She didn't want to let go of Ranvijay and his memory. And most importantly, she didn't want her husband's life and his brutal murder to have been in vain. She wanted to contribute to the cause to which Ranvijay had dedicated his life. She wanted to take that cause ahead, to make it her own. She wanted to follow his passion, his duty.

So, Meera stood up, squared her shoulders and laid it on the line: 'I've decided that I'm going to join the Indian Army.'

There was silence in the room. She saw blank astonishment on the faces in front of her. She allowed her words to sink in.

Long seconds ticked by in a bewildered silence.

'What?' thundered Ranvijay's dad, utter disbelief in his voice. Meera inhaled sharply.

'I'm going to join the Indian Army. Like Ranvijay,' she said, slowly and with emphasis on each word. 'I've spent many days and nights thinking about what I should do with this life without Ranvijay in it. For months I had no answers, and I couldn't handle the truth that he's gone, never to return. I've spent hours trying to understand what made Ranvijay pick a career that required him to put his duty before his life. And while I may never get the answer to this question, I have faith in him. I have faith in the path he took. And I want to take the same path to continue his journey, to carry his legacy forward and to work towards the same goal that he did. So yes, I will join the Indian Army, I will fight terrorists and I will follow in Ranvijay's footsteps. His path is my path now. I hope that all of you will support me, but even if you don't, I am going to do it regardless. This is my decision, and I will stand by it. This is my way of honouring Ranvijay.'

After several more moments of silence, Ranvijay's mother asked, 'Like Ranvijay?'

Clearly, they were all confused. Meera, a girl, to join the Indian Army? Was that even possible?

'Yes, Mumma, like Ranvijay,' Meera nodded.

'Are you mad, Meera?' her father demanded. 'Girls don't join the army to fight.'

'Will you become a doctor in the army?' to Meera's mother, the only way women joined the army was as doctors. Was Meera going to study medicine now, she wondered.

'I'll join the army as an officer, Ma.'

'Is it even possible?' Ranvijay's mom asked the room, looking pale.

'Yes, it's possible, Mumma,' replied Meera. 'I'll appear for the SSB and get selected in OTA—that's the training academy for women cadets. I need to train there for a year and then I can get commissioned in the army as an officer. I have checked several credible sources. I am eligible to appear this year.'

'But, beta, what will you do in the army? You're an engineer,' Meera's mother sounded baffled.

'Ma, the army needs various skill sets for its various arms, and engineering is a skill to which they recruit. I've done my research; I'm sure I'll be a good fit for their requirements.'

'Meera, I don't know what to say or what to do, beta ...' Ranvijay's mother said, close to tears.

'Give me your blessings, Mumma. Like you gave to Ranvijay,' Meera said warmly, and put a comforting hand on her shoulder.

'But Ranvijay is not here, is he?' Ranvijay's dad spoke for the first time since she had broken the news to them. Looking into Meera's eyes, he continued, 'Beta, we have lost one child already. We can't send another one to the same fate. I don't have it in me, Meera beta. I don't ...' and with this, Ranvijay's dad broke down. Annoyed at himself for showing a weak emotion, he rose and started to leave the room.

'I cannot support this either,' Meera's father declared and stood up as well. 'You come home with us right now, Meera. Staying cooped up in that room is making you go crazy. You need to live outside your fantasies and return to the real world. Put an end to this unrealistic dream. You're a widow, beta. Live a life that is suitable for you, and maybe after a year or so of Ranvijay's passing, you can go back to Pune and work. But this joining the army business is not going to happen, not under my watch.'

'I am not going crazy, Papa,' replied Meera. 'I'm not going anywhere with you and let me make something very clear right now: I am NOT a widow—I am a Veer Nari. My husband gave the supreme sacrifice fighting for this country, for you and for me, until his last breath. I'm not going to let his sacrifice be in vain. I'm not going to let a label define me and I'll prove to be a *veer* even in this state of grief.'

Her father gaped at her. On some level, he had always been aware of Meera's obduracy towards his outdated beliefs and set ways, but this was the first time he was seeing the fire in her eyes burn so bright.

'And lastly, Papa,' Meera went on calmly, like they were discussing the weather, 'nothing I do is "happening under your watch". I am my own person; I get to decide my life on my own terms—that is what Ranvijay instilled in me. I will join the Indian Army, and that is final, whether you support me or not.'

'Then you're on your own. I do not support this madness and I want nothing to do with you,' Meera's father said, tears of disappointment shining in his eyes. *Why does this child of mine make everything unnecessarily tough*? he wondered in despair.

The answer to this question, which he didn't know at the time, was that *Meera* was tough. That day, even as he denounced Meera's radical decision and then stormed out of Ranvijay's parents' house, his quiet wife in tow, he knew in his heart that Meera would do what she was determined to do. There were no two ways about it. If Meera set her mind on something, no matter how unrealistic, her father knew that she would give it her all. He only wished that she wouldn't follow through on this one because, to his mind, the army was no life for a lady. She wouldn't be able to keep up and would probably end up getting hurt even more by her own failure.

'It's all right, Papa,' he heard Meera say as he walked away, 'it may be madness to you, but I'm going to do it, with or without your support.' He didn't turn around even when Ranvijay's father followed after him, calling out his name.

Back in the room, Ranvijay's mom sat still and silently in her seat. She hadn't moved throughout all this drama.

'Mumma?' Meera said, kneeling on the floor beside her sofa. She put her hand on the older woman's shoulder gently.

'Is there any way you will reconsider this decision, beta?' Ranvijay's mom asked in a whisper.

Meera shook her head.

'In that case, let me help you prepare for the SSB test. I know you'll come out with flying colours in the written test—if there is a written test, that is. But I've been through the physical-fitness test with Ranvijay during his time, so I know a thing or two about preparing for it and I'm going to help you start—'

Meera hugged her before she could finish her sentence. Both of them began to cry.

'I know from where Ranvijay got his kindness and selflessness, Mumma,' said Meera, wiping her tears after a few moments. 'From you. He got all his best qualities from you.'

Ranvijay's mother brushed her hand over Meera's head, tucking some loose strands of hair behind her ears in the typical, achingly loving way that only mothers do.

'You have my blessings, beta. Just as Ranvijay did. And I also wish you luck, stronger and better than what Ranvijay had. It is a noble path, although it's probably the toughest one for parents to see their kids take, especially for someone like me, a mother who has already lost her son. But it is a noble path. Soldiers are cut from an entirely different cloth altogether and I know you'll be the best of the best.'

Meera began to tear up again. She thanked her stars for having this kind, loving and, most importantly, strong woman in her life.

* * *

Strength of character is not a linear concept, Meera learned that day. It was a complex one. In some of us, this strength is visible from the get-go, out there for the world to see. But in a few of us, it makes itself known under duress, in circumstances that test a person's mettle. And it takes others by surprise, because it isn't apparent, it isn't loud and it isn't flamboyant. People who possess this type of silent strength of character often shine like a beacon in the darkest hour for their loved ones who need it the most.

Meera's mother-in-law was one such person. Her faith in Meera was bulletproof, and there was nothing more that Meera wanted than for someone to believe in her like Ranvijay did.

So, at the end of this long day, Meera discovered that it was her warm, loving and soft-spoken mother-in-law who had proved to be her staunch and steadfast ally.

And that was that. Meera didn't look back. Some relatives from both sides of the family tried to talk her out of it, using fear or shame as a tactic. While a few others sounded vaguely in awe of her decision, no one was sure if the path she had chosen was the 'right' thing to do for a widow. No one could tell whether Meera was delusional or brave in wanting to join the army as a lady officer.

No one, except Meera herself.

In fact, she had never been so sure of anything in her life. Even the decision to marry Ranvijay all those years ago seemed like a run-up to this exact moment.

After months of feeling guilty of taking too much space in a world where Ranvijay was no more, this was the first time Meera felt like she belonged.

14

The next day, Meera had an unexpected visitor.

Her mother arrived in an autorickshaw. It was around noon, so Meera knew that her father would be at work, just as her father-in-law was. After serving tea and snacks, Ranvijay's mother discreetly excused herself so Meera could talk to her mother in private and sort out what had transpired the previous evening.

Meera took her mother upstairs to her room. They sat together in the balcony, sipping tea and talking about the weather. Then, Meera couldn't take the small talk any more, 'Ma, I'm sorry if my decision makes you unhappy or puts you at loggerheads with Papa,' she held her mother's hands in hers. 'I wish I were easy. I wish I weren't an embarrassment to Papa. But I am; and I'm okay with that, because who am I if I don't pursue my purpose in life?'

Meera's mother stayed silent for a while, tenderly caressing her daughter's hands. She remembered holding a tiny Meera for the first time, a few seconds after giving birth to her. Meera had decided to come into the world a full three weeks earlier than expected, with a body weight far lower than normal for a healthy child. She was held in the neonatal intensive care unit for a week, but she was a fighter and had thrived and gained weight faster than had been expected by the amazed doctors. Meera's mother remembered what a fighter Meera had been since the very beginning of her precious life. And, as she grew, she continued to fight: against the norms, for what she believed in and for her place in a world where girls were loved but not treated as equals.

Yes, Meera's mother had decided, her daughter was a fighter and it was time to support her so that she had one more person in her corner. That was why she was here today.

'Your decision makes me really proud of you, Meera. The more I think about how you told us about it last evening, about what you're going to accomplish, it fills me with pride to be your mother, beta.'

'Ma, are you serious?'

'I am. And I'm sorry that I didn't show you my support immediately, but I'm here now, to tell you that you have my blessing, my support and my love.'

'Ma,' Meera felt the tears prick at her eyes.

'And, Meera, you have to know that you're not an embarrassment to us. You make us so proud. Even if your father is overprotective of you at the moment and terrified to leave you out in the cold, alone in this big world, both of us acknowledge the inner strength you have, and we thank God for it every day. To go through what you're going through with Ranvijay's passing . . . Meera, not many people would have endured it and come out with a resolve so positive and strong that it scares us. I'm proud of you.'

Meera hugged her mother thinking about how the women in this family—her mother-in-law and her mother—both had surprised her with their strength of character and unconditional love.

It made Meera's heart full and her determination, stronger.

Meera worked hard from that day onwards, not caring that her father wasn't speaking to her or that her father-in-law seemed almost certain that she wouldn't get into the academy. Her father-in-law had actually expressed it a couple of times, although mildly, that what she was preparing for was one of the toughest entrance tests to crack. Meera would've felt insulted, had she stopped to care about it. She was too busy working hard to make the cut because Ranvijay's father was right: SSB was one of the toughest tests to crack. It was designed in a way that tested not only the academic prowess of a candidate, but also his or her mental boundaries. Meera had to work hard.

And she did.

For the next few months, Meera forgot all about her life outside of this dream. She gave it her all. Both the mothers helped her in every way possible, while both fathers remained distant and disapproving.

One unexpectedly good thing that happened was that, upon the suggestion of her mother-in-law, Meera called to inform Ranvijay's CO about her decision to try for the upcoming SSB entry, and the news was enthusiastically received. The CO promised her all his help and guidance, and further assured her that he would inform the relevant authorities as well—a Veer Nari aspiring to join the forces was a rare thing in those days, and he was immensely proud of her for nurturing that dream and having the strength and conviction to follow it through, irrespective of the result.

She had planned to call Capt. Rana later, but he had called her within half an hour, nearly out of breath with excitement.

He too was supportive like the CO had been, 'The entire paltan knows, Meera,' he chuckled when she asked him how he had found out, 'and everyone is celebrating.'

'No pressure on me then, phew!' Meera joked.

Capt. Rana laughed. Then he asked her a serious question.

'Why do you want to join the army, Meera?'

It was a straightforward question, and Meera wanted to answer it honestly.

'You're asking why would a war widow, a Veer Nari, want to tread on the same career path that got her husband killed in the first place, right?'

'Yes . . .'

'There are many reasons a Veer Nari would want to join the army, Capt. Rana. And those reasons can differ from person to person, situation to situation,' Meera explained. 'But at the heart of it, the main reasons remain the same for each war widow who feels like I do, and wants to join the Indian Army in the footsteps of their late husbands who gave the supreme sacrifice: To feel closer to the departed husband. To honour his legacy. And to carry forward the dream that he had.'

Capt. Rana remained silent, taking in her words. Meera continued.

'And personally, for me, I want to join the Indian Army to find the purpose of this life . . . a life which I somehow still have, and Ranvijay doesn't. To make better use of these days in which I'm alive, when he isn't.'

'That's . . .' Capt. Rana trailed off. What could he say to this determined, young girl that would do justice to the enormous swell of pride he was feeling right now. Words were not enough. He kept quiet. Meera spoke again.

'I don't know if this is a childish pipedream, Rana bhai-sa,' Meera confessed, 'but I will give it my all. There's no plan B for me.'

'Spoken like a true fauji already, Meera!' Capt. Rana said. 'I'm here, always available if you need my help.'

'I'm counting on it,' said Meera, 'Capt. Vikram Rana.'

'Why the full name?' asked Capt. Rana.

'Now that I'm going to be an army officer, I will have to address you as a senior officer should be addressed,' Meera reasoned.

'There's a long way to go before the commissioning, Meera,' Capt. Rana laughed, 'but I'm glad to see that your josh is high. I'm going to help you along the journey to the best of my abilities, Meera.' And true to his word, he was of constant support to Meera: from helping her with her studies to giving her useful tips about the SSB. As did the CO and the then 2IC, Lt Col Iyer.

The officers were a huge help to Meera in more ways than one: apart from helping her prepare for her exam, being in touch with them made Meera feel closer to Ranvijay. It was difficult for her to explain but staying connected with them kept her going, kept her motivated. She gave it her all, as promised. There really wasn't a plan B.

Meera quit Infosys and began to study diligently for hours on end. She also trained physically as much as she could, to build up her stamina. While she had always been a bright student and was physically fit and in shape, she knew that she would need to build her endurance and stamina even more. So, she joined an SSB coaching academy in Bikaner which was run by a veteran officer. She was glad that her savings from her Infosys salary allowed her to pay for the help she needed. It was like she was slowly seeing God's larger plan for her emerge.

***

January 2015

Meera had appeared for the written test for CDS OTA in September and had just been told that she had cleared it. She was elated, but the road stretched ahead of her, long and arduous, because, after the written exam, came the SSB, which was probably one of the most difficult interviews to crack. While she was waiting for her SSB dates and to find out the SSB centre assigned to her, another news arrived.

Lt Col Iyer called Meera one morning and told her that it had just been announced that Ranvijay was being given the Kirti Chakra posthumously. He gave her more information about the selection process, the protocols to receive the award and how the CO would be there with her at the time of the facilitation, as per tradition. Meera was too stunned to make sense of anything. She wordlessly handed the phone to her mother-in-law, and sat there, staring into space.

Meera knew that the Kirti Chakra was the peacetime equivalent of the Maha Vir Chakra. Ranvijay had been a

Sena Medal awardee already, and he had once told Meera that very soon he would be Sena Medal Bar—which meant he would be a double Sena Medal awardee. Remembering these snippets of life with him was always painful for Meera; grief would often engulf her for hours and she would sit in her room, crying in secret; as she again did on that day.

The days to the day of the award flew by in a blur. Meera travelled to Delhi for the ceremony a couple of days prior, with Ranvijay's parents. On 26 January 2015, Meera wore a white linen saree, gathered her hair back in a ponytail and sat in an army Gypsy that took her and her in-laws to the Republic Day parade ground. Oblivious to the hustle and bustle of the parade, Meera sat still on her chair, staring into nothingness. *This used to be the emotional scene from the war movies*, she thought. *This is my life now.*

When the time came, Ranvijay's Para SF unit's CO, who was seated beside her and her family, ushered her towards the enclosure where the President of India stood, along with other dignitaries. She walked with Ranvijay's CO on her left, marching up to the mark on the carpet as per prior instructions, and stood there as Ranvijay's name was announced.

'Capt. Ranvijay Chauhan. Para SF. Posthumously,' the voice announced.

Don't cry, don't cry here—Meera repeated to herself in her mind. She needed to get through this.

The announcement continued: 'In April 2014, Capt. Ranvijay Chauhan was assigned a mission in Jammu and Kashmir's Kupwara district, to intercept a group of terrorists crossing . . .'

Meera's mind went blank at this point, almost like she had slipped into a trance, and she could only hear a faint buzz. She stood there, expressionless, not knowing where to look or how to be in that moment. She stood there as the voice on the audio system continued to recount Ranvijay's final operation.

'... for displaying commendable leadership and bravery, thereby eliminating three heavily armed terrorists, for displaying exemplary heroism, selflessness and intrepidity at the risk of his life above and beyond the call of duty in the highest traditions of Para SF, Capt. Ranvijay Chauhan is awarded of Kirti Chakra (posthumously).'

At this, Meera's resolve broke a bit and although not one emotion showed on her face, a single tear rolled down her cheek.

'Late Capt. Ranvijay Chauhan's wife, Mrs Meera Chauhan,' the announcement concluded, as the President walked over to her and handed her the medal. Cameras flashed and Meera felt more lost than ever in the middle of this celebration of Ranvijay's bravery and heroism. Was it a celebration if he wasn't here for it, she thought. No, it wasn't, a voice in her head said, she walked away with the CO marching beside her.

The award ceremony, like the entire Republic Day parade in India, was telecast live across various TV channels and the Internet. Within hours, the video clip of a devastated Meera standing before the President to receive the Kirti Chakra on behalf of her husband, as the announcer described her husband's final operation when he was killed in action, became a visual that moved the nation.

The young, petite girl in a white saree, looking lost and still very much in mourning, led to several debates and panel discussions about war widows. One channel even started a drive to spread awareness about the struggles of Veer Naris. And the visual of that one teardrop on Meera's stoic face, haunted the nation for days.

But Meera had no time for theatrics. She finally had her letter for SSB in Bangalore. She began preparing for it with renewed gusto, not worrying at all about any narratives or drives.

15

March 2015

It was Meera's first day at the Officer's Training Academy in Chennai.

She had done it!

After months and months of hard work, she had cleared the SSB—the meticulously planned, rigorous test to separate the wheat from the chaff and select the crème de la crème of those who had cleared the written exams. Meera read somewhere that success rate in the SSB was an alarming 2 per cent. But she was prepared, she was determined and she gave her best at each task and every test. On the fourth day of the SSB interview process, during what was being called a 'conference', Meera's name was announced, and it took her a full minute to realize that she had been selected. In a group of about 250 candidates, she was one of the four selected! They were instructed to report at 6 a.m. the following day for medicals.

Thrilled to bits and choked with emotion, she telephoned Ranvijay's mother from Bangalore to give her the good news; but Ranvijay's father had answered the call.

'*Haan*, beta?' he said. 'Your Mumma has gone for a walk and left her mobile phone at home,' he said awkwardly. Although he had never once behaved rudely to Meera, there was still discomfort between them. After a pause, Meera decided to share the news with him.

'Dad, I got through,' she said.

'What?!'

'I got through SSB, Dad. They just announced the results.'

'Beta—' he began, but Meera cut him off, because she didn't want to hear anything that would dampen the extreme excitement that she was feeling right now.

'Dad, they only selected four women from this batch of 250 hopeful candidates,' she said. 'I am one of the four cadets selected! I made it! I made the cut! And if the Indian Army thinks I'm worthy, maybe I am.'

'You *are* worthy, *mera baccha*,' she heard her father-in-law say at the other end of the line. 'You've always been worthy of whatever dream you held, Meera. I never doubted you, even when I did not support you,' he continued.

'Dad, I know I haven't been the ideal *bahu* to you, but I want you to know that your support would mean a lot to me,' Meera couldn't stop herself from saying.

'I didn't support your decision to join the army not because of any orthodox notion, beta. I couldn't support it because I lost my son to this path, and I didn't want to lose another child. You are not a bahu to me, Meera beta, you are like my own child. And I was scared, I still am.'

'Dad . . .' Meera wiped hot tears from her cheeks. Her father-in-law continued.

'But now I know that my fears shouldn't be a barrier to you. You've chosen the path of a yoddha, Meera beta and I want you to know that I'm proud of you. Just as proud as I am of Ranvijay,' Meera heard him choke back a sob.

Ranvijay would've loved to hear this, she thought. She thanked her father-in-law, called her mother to give her the news as well and returned to the room assigned to her at the SSB centre, to mentally prepare herself for the next steps.

Over the next few days, Meera appeared for the various medical tests that are an important part of the SSB selection process, and she sailed through them. By the end of the week, Meera was officially selected for training as a lady cadet for the next session at Officers Training Academy (OTA) in Chennai.

* * *

After a tearful yet giddy goodbye at the Bikaner railway station to her mother and her in-laws—her father had still not come to terms with her decision—she was now finally at the mighty campus of OTA, Chennai, with her backpack and a trunk, in typical fauji fashion. The black metal trunk still had Ranvijay's name written on it. She had been meaning to paint her own name over it, but she hadn't been able to bring herself to do it.

It was still dark outside, and Meera was sitting on the floor beside her—Ranvijay's—trunk. Wiping the hot tears from her face, she ran a hand along the white writing on the black trunk.

Capt. Ranvijay Chauhan | PARA SF

Her assigned roommate, cadet Simran Sandhu, was perched on her single bed at the opposite end of the room, and was watching her.

They had stayed up all night talking because neither of them could sleep with all the excitement of having made it to OTA. They had ended up discussing each other's journeys to the academy.

Simran was from Chandigarh and belonged to a business family; but she had always wanted to join the forces since very early in her life. Her family hadn't understood this ambition: traditionally, sons had joined the business and daughters had married business partners to grow the business and have a safe, cushioned life of lavish homes and frequent international holidays. Why would she want to break away from a life of such luxury and comfort? But Simran had been adamant. She wanted something different for herself.

Like Meera, getting into OTA was a dream come true for Simran. One of her seniors from college in Chandigarh was a few courses ahead of them in OTA and had given Simran a first-hand download of the life of a lady cadet in the academy that accepted nothing but complete commitment and excellence in every field.

'The Indian Army is not one of the world's most capable and feared armies for nothing,' she had said to Simran when she had called to share the news of her selection. 'It is the way it is because it doesn't accept mediocrity in any form. So be ready to face a new demon every day. The academy is not for the weak, so keep going until you fall down. And when you fall down, take a beat, and stand up again. All the best!'

Simran narrated this verbatim to Meera, and while both of them had known that training to be an Indian Army officer wasn't going to be a cake walk, this reinforced it. The next eleven months were going to show them their limits and hopefully, ways to conquer those limits.

'The fight is only just starting and will carry on until we wear the stars on our shoulders, my friend,' said Simran. 'And then, there'll be a new fight—for me, it will be to defy the thinking of my family, and for you, to honour that name painted on that trunk.'

Simran raised her glass of water towards Meera, in a toast to their new beginning. Meera picked up her bottle of water and raised it in Simran's direction in reply. She knew it was early days yet and that she wasn't here to make friends, but something told Meera that she had made a real friend.

Both gulped down some water and giggled before rushing to get ready for the drill. No matter what each of their journeys had been up until then, in this room, both future lady officers felt at home with each other and eagerly looked forward to their training.

Until the next day happened.

16

The cadets were asked to report to the parade ground at 4.30 a.m., in their brand-new, tailored, combat uniforms. The uniforms were heavy, and the lady cadets were sweating despite the relatively cool morning in Chennai's otherwise high-humidity climate.

Their drill *ustaad* was already standing in the ground, waiting. Over the last couple of days, the lady cadets had been introduced to their company commanders and some of their instructors for this training. There would be senior officers training them in academics; there would be junior officers working as instructors across various streams and subjects focusing on cadets in smaller groups; and highly trained and experienced soldiers—called 'ustaads'—who were responsible for their physical, on-ground training.

And this particular drill ustaad, standing there, sharply dressed in his uniform complete with a maroon beret, had no expression whatsoever on his face or in his eyes.

'Ten laps around the ground,' the ustaad's voice boomed at 4.37 a.m., startling the cadets who were still in the process of forming orderly lines. This was punishment because the cadets were late in assembling—they ought to have been ready at 4.30 a.m., on the dot—and tardiness was not tolerated around here.

'Are we late?' Simran muttered under her breath to Meera. 'Did we just get ourselves ten laps for being seven minutes late? What would've happened had we been ten minutes late? What kind of math is this?'

Meera suppressed a giggle.

'Fifteen rounds to the two cadets in row number two,' the ustaad commanded, looking directly at Simran and Meera.

'What?' Simran squeaked, realizing that the ustaad was looking at them.

'Eighteen.'

'But we were just—'

'Twenty,' snapped the ustad, his voice now angry.

Meera grabbed Simran's hand before she could blurt out anything more and earned them both more rounds around this vast, VAST ground, and started running.

Ten extra laps as punishment for the two of them.

'Not a great start to the training,' Meera muttered to Simran, who was already out of breath by the eighth round. 'Let us both try to speak less and listen more from now on.'

'And let us try to be on time,' managed Simran, clutching her stomach.

Both the girls pushed themselves to finish the added punishment as quickly as they could manage.

'Welcome to OTA,' the ustaad addressed them all after they had finished their ten laps around the periphery of the ground—twenty for Meera and Simran. He made the remaining cadets jog nonstop in place while they waited for girls. No wonder everyone looked angrily at the two of them.

'My name is Havaldar Manoj Kumar and I am your drill ustaad. All of you will be trained here. Here, you will learn to love this country and the passion to be ready to die for your country will also be inculcated in you. You have all become cadets from being regular girls, but here you will train to be officers from cadets—and this road is not easy. Only those who emerge like shining gold from the fires of the forge will see victory,' thundered the ustaad to the group.

Upon hearing this, the sea of sweating and out-of-breath faces in the lines before him shone with joyful anticipation—and amazement that they had managed to make it this far. It was an achievement indeed to be selected in SSB; they knew they were the cream of the crop.

But the joy of accomplishment was tempered with fear of what they knew was to come: days filled with hard work, sweat, blood, toil and tears; days that would require them to prove that they were worthy of being a part of the world's best army; and days that were sure to test the endurance limits of each and every cadet.

Just then, as if on cue, a cadet to their right threw up and then passed out. The drill ustaad was unfazed, 'You people have no strength or stamina. You'll have to work very hard. You'll need to train your brain so that the body doesn't give up until the mind tells it to. And when will the mind tell the body to give up?' the ustaad demanded, pacing up and down in measured steps along the row of cadets. He stopped before the cadet who was lying unconscious on the ground, breathing loudly. After a pause, he repeated his question: 'And when will the mind tell the body to give up?'

Silence from the cadets met his question, as a medical assistant knelt by the cadet who had fainted from exhaustion on day one of physical training.

'WHEN WILL THE MIND TELL THE BODY TO GIVE UP?' the instructor's voice reverberated.

'Sir . . .' a cadet spoke up.

'Ustaad!' he cut her off before she could say another word. 'You will all address me as ustaad.'

'Ustaad,' the cadet tried again, 'when the enemy is defeated, only then will the mind tell the body to give up.'

'WRONG!' bellowed Ustaad and all the cadets shook a little at the force of his voice.

'The mind will *never* tell the body to give up. NEVER. You will go on to become officers of the Indian Army, and your mind will *never* tell the body to give up. You will train your mind for *sada vijay*—meaning victory, always. This is your aim for the duration of this training.'

'Ji, Ustaad,' everyone chorused in unison, in awe of what they had just heard. His words had evoked many emotions in the cadets, including Meera.

I will train my brain for sada vijay, always victory, she thought to herself. And as she glanced around at the faces of her fellow cadets, as they jogged back to their rooms to change and head to classes, she realized that every resolute face reflected that same determination.

* * *

The first few weeks in the academy flew past like a whirlwind, and Meera—like all her course mates—barely had time to catch her breath. Meera remained single-mindedly dedicated to her training and academics, but she did make a few other friends besides Simran. Most of them belonged to the same company as her, Zojila Company.

The cadets were divided into equal groups in every course and were assigned to 'companies' for better management and learning. Each company had its own legacy and was often a matter of pride for the cadets, a pride that needed to be upheld by winning every competition in the academy. Needless to say, it kept the cadets motivated. Going forward in their careers, academy companies were also like niche communities that gave a sense of belonging to officers for years to come.

Hearing about the lives of some of the other girls in her course, Meera realized that, while the details and the threads were different in each case, at the core of every story was struggle and stubbornness.

This realization made her feel even more at home at the academy. Everyone had had their challenges, and this group training with her here at the OTA had conquered and overcome all their hurdles to be where they were today. *What an accomplished bunch of girls I am with*, Meera thought with joy and admiration.

But soon, something started to bother Meera.

Meera realized that a lot of her course-mates knew her story and her background—they knew about Ranvijay and obviously knew she was a Veer Nari. This made Meera uncomfortable because she didn't want any pity from her course mates during the training. She had asked Ranvijay's

CO to help her by requesting the academy and its board on her behalf about keeping her background and story confidential. The CO had confirmed that the academy had not only agreed to her request but were actually in favour of keeping it from becoming general knowledge. The reason given to her was straightforward: the OTA management board acknowledged that Meera made the cut based on her own capabilities and they believed that Meera deserved equal credit and opportunity as the other cadets. So, the academy supported her desire to not let Ranvijay and his martyrdom cast any sort of unnecessary judgement or bearing on her academy training.

What Meera didn't know was that the Indian Defence Ministry had been keeping tabs on her ever since she had cleared the OTA entrance examination. While no influence could sway the decisions of the SSB's selection board and Meera got through purely on merit, the ministry wanted to ensure Meera's safety. She was a young war widow whose husband was killed by one of the most brutal terrorist chiefs in the world, in an ambush custom-designed for him. What had happened to Ranvijay was a personal vendetta, orchestrated to issue a statement, and even though the details were censored and withheld from the media, it had made a huge splash in news channels and publications across the country. Video footage of a sobbing Meera receiving the tricolour that draped Ranvijay's coffin on the day of his funeral had run on loop on various TV channels and social media for a week. Needless to say, Meera's was the latest Veer Nari whose story had garnered the nation's sympathy and support in the recent times, and she could prove to be a substantial target if any anti-national forces wanted to instigate national outrage and unrest. If there were even a slim chance of Lashkar targeting Meera, the Indian defence machinery wanted to prevent it. Also, Indian intelligence suspected that, if news of Capt. Ranvijay Chauhan's wife joining the army were to leak out, Khayyam might do something, if only to make another statement.

Therefore, the ministry had been regularly tracking her SSB progress. When they learnt that Meera had requested anonymity, the ministry not only wholeheartedly supported it but also ensured that her background be kept a secret from other cadets and from the public in general. This was for her own safety. They didn't want to sacrifice another valuable life in a terrorist's revenge plot or his power play.

What had been done to Capt. Ranvijay still sent shivers down the collective spine of the department. The way Khayyam had sought him out and taken revenge so cold bloodedly and in such a gruesome way—everything pointed towards hatred that went far deeper than politics, religion or territory.

All Meera knew was that Ranvijay's CO had spoken to the OTA commandant, who had agreed to grant Meera her wish of being treated like any other cadet.

So, when she realized that some of the cadets knew who she was, it felt like an unnecessary burden on her.

'Capt. Ranvijay's story was covered by the news channels a lot,' Simran had offered, trying to comfort Meera. 'Your video of receiving his Kirti Chakra posthumously became so popular that I wouldn't be surprised if some channels still play it on every Republic Day for ratings. Some channels ran your pictures at the last rites at the time, as well. Those clips and images were all over social media, Meera. And you know that what's on social media never really dies, even if a lot of time has passed.'

'You're right,' Meera had agreed begrudgingly. 'Don't get me wrong, I am not trying to disassociate from Ranvijay. He's the reason I'm here in the first place, I'm proud to be his wife. I just want to be treated like every other cadet here, that's all. I just feel that once people know that I'm a Veer Nari, they either have suspicion in their eyes, because *why would a girl who has already suffered so much from the death of her husband join the army for more torture*, or worse, pity.'

Simran nodded in understanding.

'I just want to be able to keep my head down and do my best until we pass out and get commissioned. I don't want to be dealing with people's pity or their doubts about my abilities or intentions.'

'Understandable.'

'Story of my life—dealing with unnecessary obstacles and for no reason at all,' Meera sighed loudly and melodramatically, and Simran laughed.

'It'll be all right. You'll handle it, this much I know about you in this short time span, Cadet Chauhan,' Simran flung an encouraging arm around Meera. 'If anyone can do this, it's you.'

Meera laughed and bent down to pull on her sports shoes. Together, they jogged towards the mess for dinner, for which they had exactly eighteen minutes. Life moved with the needles of the clock here, and twenty-four hours just didn't seem enough.

17

Two-and-a-half months into the training, Meera's batch got its first liberty. A liberty is permission for cadets—who lived and trained in the same campus 24/7—to venture out of the academy for a few hours. It was a Sunday, and Meera had decided to stay back at the campus to practise some parts of her physical training. While she was doing well in academics, maintaining one of the top three spots in all subjects and was just as good at map reading and tactics, she was struggling with physical training. Although she was healthy and had commendable stamina, she still wasn't up to the mark—and the ustaad told her that every day, without fail. Not only was it humiliating to be hauled up regularly, it also made Meera terrified about not clearing her physical tests that were a must before being commissioned. So, today, she didn't leave the campus on liberty and headed to the training ground instead.

After a few rigorous rounds of an obstacle course—her main enemy, which she hadn't yet conquered as well as she hoped to—Meera headed to her room to crash for a couple of hours. Sleep was a luxury in the academy; the cadets never got enough of it.

Looking forward to her snooze, Meera returned to her room to see Simran sitting there, crying.

'Arrey, what happened?' she asked and sat down beside Simran on the floor, gently patting her on her back to soothe her.

'My mom and dad are coming down to meet me,' Simran managed between sobs.

'Here? In Chennai? From Chandigarh?' Meera asked. 'But why are you crying?'

'They're getting me engaged to someone!' Simran cried, tears flowing afresh down her face.

'What the—' Meera muttered. This didn't make any sense.

She discovered that Simran's parents had come to Chennai along with long-time family friends and hopefully future business partners.

'Chandigarh se Chennai, with the boy—wow!' exclaimed Meera.

'My mom will come to the bloody LOC between active shelling to get me married, if it comes to that,' Simran said miserably. 'She's completely obsessed with marrying me off so that I can snap out of my "army phase".'

'She thinks it's a phase?' Meera was incredulous. 'You've been here for almost three months, training your ass off!'

'Unbelievable, no?' Simran said. 'I cleared the country's toughest entrance exam, and she still thinks what I *really* want is a profitable marriage deal? I mean, even Amitabh Bachchan didn't get through SSB, and I did! I did, Meera!

But it's still just a "silly phase" to her. It's so humiliating to have your own parents not give a shit about your dreams.'

'I know what that feels like,' said Meera. A child— no matter how old—always craves for validation and acceptance from the parents. The absence of it creates a void. Meera knew all about that: her own father hadn't spoken to her since the day she had announced her plan to join the Indian Army. And while it did break her heart, it hadn't affected her as much as it might have because of the two stalwart women back home who provided a solid support system for her.

'I want to do this, Meera,' Simran began sobbing again. 'You know I'm capable.'

'Of course, you are,' said Meera. 'And I know this is not some "phase". So, get up, wash your face and stand your ground when your parents get here. *Chalo* cadet, get up,' she said, imitating the ustaad's loud voice.

Simran smiled through her tears at the poor attempt at mimicry. 'I won't succumb to her emotional blackmail this time,' said Simran resolutely, as she got to her feet. 'The time to test the mind's training to never give up is here, Meera,' she said in a way that made Meera laugh.

'Now that's more like it!' said Meera. '*Har maidan fateh* (conquer every battlefield)!' declared Meera, imitating Simran and making her laugh as well.

Meera was confident that her tough Punjabi friend would handle the situation and come back from the meeting triumphant and happy. So, she wished Simran all the best as she set off to face her ordeal, dressed in a kurta and jeans—a deliberate rebellion against her mother who had specifically instructed Simran to wear an elaborate Punjabi suit with dupatta—and caught up on her sleep.

By the time she woke up, Simran was back after saying a firm no to her parents for the engagement and wedding.

'I did spend more time than I intended to, having coffee with Sunny, though,' Simran admitted with a wink. 'He's not bad, you know. He's doing his MBA in finance and will probably get a job in an MNC instead of doing that *faltoo* fabrics *ka* business like the rest of his family. He has dreams of moving to one of the Nordic countries, you know,' she said dreamily.

'Oh, I see,' Meera teased. 'Someone is in L-O-V-E!'

'Not at all! I won't let anything distract me from my training.'

'But the training will end in nine months,' Meera pointed out with a naughty smile.

'We'll handle it when the time comes, *yaar*!' Simran said and the girls laughed.

'But seriously, though, do you like him?' Meera inquired while they were having lunch.

Simran thought about it and then said, 'I guess he surprised me—by not being the stereotypical Punjabi business-family heir, as I had expected. He was well-spoken, had basic manners and all that. But I think what I liked the most about him was the fact that he had ambition outside of his family's money.'

This made Meera miss Ranvijay.

She nodded in honest understanding and kept her head down, focusing on her food so that she could avoid the emotional hurricane that she knew was lurking around the corner, just waiting for a weak moment. She missed Ranvijay multiple times on most days, but she had been missing him more so since the previous evening. There was no significant reason for this, except the fact that one of the instructors, to whom she had been speaking about her class, had mentioned to her that Ranvijay had been his junior in NDA and had told her how proud he was of Meera. The instructor had meant well, and probably intended to just be encouraging, but it made her grief emerge from the shadows, where she kept it hidden, and engulf her.

But she couldn't let her emotions overwhelm her, not now, not during this training. She was determined to be a cut above the rest, so she pushed aside the heavy feeling and soldiered on.

* * *

A few days later, Meera got a letter from Ranvijay's mother.

The cadets didn't have the time to surf the Internet, but neither Ma nor her mumma were all that Internet-savvy to send emails anyway, so they wrote letters to her: physical, handwritten letters, which she loved.

This particular letter made her tear up, though. Her mother-in-law had written that Ranvijay was mentally strong even as a little boy and had gone on to describe an incident from when he was eight years old. He had just recovered from a week-long bout of seasonal viral fever which had left him very weak, she wrote. But, on Republic Day, he participated in a school race because the prize was a state-of-the-art video game set, the kind you could plug into your television, and which came with thirty-six different games installed in it, with a fancy controller and everything. It was something he had been asking his parents for a long time. They had been reluctant to buy it for him because they felt video games, at such a young age, were not good.

So, when he realized he had a chance of getting what he wanted, he went for it in full swing. He was still very weak, but he put all his strength into the run and completed it in first place, only to fall unconscious the moment he crossed the finishing line. When he regained consciousness a few minutes later, the first thing he said was, 'I won! Bring me my video game!'

Meera laughed hard upon reading this, but tears pooled in her eyes at the same time. She sat at her modest desk and wrote back to her mother-in-law: *I wish I had the same mental strength as Ranvijay.*

She described her days at the academy to her mother-in-law. She admitted in the letter that the training was taking a toll on her because she wasn't physically strong. Runs were fine, but obstacle courses and more complex forms of training often got the better of her.

And moreover, because every day she was pushing herself beyond her limits to improve herself, her physical state was affecting her academics—something she had never had trouble with before.

She needed to be mentally stronger to be able to finish top of her class, she wrote in the letter.

She also wrote that she sometimes felt out of place in this course, because she was here for a different reason and that made her feel like she stuck out like a sore thumb. Every cadet in the course was here because of their passion for the country, their inherent need to do more with their lives, to fight for a cause bigger than themselves. Some were here because they were following in the glorious footsteps of their father and brothers, generations of fauji blood in them and some others were here because they wanted to devote their life to a noble cause, break free of the shackles of familial expectations which society imposes on girls their age.

But Meera was different, she was here after her husband was martyred. She was a Veer Nari. Although her reasons were broadly the same, they still seemed different to her because she had a precise motive, to serve where her brave husband had once served and had laid down his life. Loss and grief fuelled her drive to tread the same path her husband had trodden on until his last breath. The fire in her burned brighter and her hunger for excellence in the training was fiercer than most, and it was there for everyone to see.

Another problem she was facing was in the form of a specific person: their main physical training ustaad, Havaldar Manoj Kumar. He was a tough man who, according to some senior cadets, had seen combat through many years of postings in Kashmir, and had been part of several CI/CT operations carried out by the Indian Army. Rumour had it that he was once critically injured during a counterinsurgency mission in the valley, and the fact that this was his first peace posting after continuous tenures in troubled areas of Kashmir for nine years straight was proof of his dedication to the country, to his duty.

While Ustaad Manoj Kumar was known to be tough on the cadets, he was extra tough on Meera.

At times, Meera felt that Ustaad regarded her as unfit to be an officer, a studious girl from a quiet city in

Rajasthan who had never had to test her physical strength before landing in the academy. She felt that he was annoyed by her incompetence, and it made her cringe with self-loathing at times. The more she tried to do better, the more unconvinced of her abilities he seemed.

Day after day, the ustaad continued to put extra pressure on Meera, more than on any other cadet; it was something that a couple of the others noticed as well.

He was the drill ustaad and yet he would often ask Meera—only Meera, and no one else—about her shooting performance. Meera was convinced that he did this on purpose because he had somehow discovered that she was usually a wash-out in shooting and was made to roll several times after the shooting-practice results were announced. This frustrated Meera: not only was her physical state not up to the mark after these first few months in the academy, she was also not very good at shooting—a crucial skill for a soldier, regardless of the arm to which they may be assigned later on.

Every time Meera begrudgingly told him her shooting score, Ustaad Manoj Kumar would make her do extra push-ups. Often, she would be the only one in the grounds, doing push-ups as a punishment for bad shooting—after she had already been made to roll as punishment for the same offence by the shooting instructor. It only reinforced her belief that Ustaad Manoj Kumar didn't consider her fit to be an officer. Meera was sure that he was just waiting for her to break and quit the training.

'But I won't quit, Mumma. I won't let him win. Because I am training my mind to never give up. And this isn't about him anyway; this is far bigger than him or any other person who is unreasonably offended at my audacity to dream,'

Meera wrote in the letter to her mother-in-law. 'I will just need to remain strong and carry on.'

She wished she had the mental strength that an eight-year-old Ranvijay had had.

'Send me some of your strength, Mumma,' she added in the letter. 'Along with your aloo paranthas. I am tired of eating boiled eggs every day because there is never time to eat anything else!'

Then, wanting to end the letter on a positive note, she wrote, *'Jaegi to jaan jaegi, Mumma, himmat nahi* (my life could leave me, but not my courage).'

She then sealed the letter and sent it by post.

* * *

Meera continued with the routine, doing her hardest to do better, but the challenges she had written about in her letter weighed constantly on her mind.

As she went through the days, she gave herself pep-talks. She reminded herself that she had known how tough the training would be in OTA, but she was prepared! She was motivated. She also constantly reminded herself of the reason she was here in the first place and not in an air-conditioned office. She was here to walk the same path as Ranvijay and to carry his dream forward. She could not fail. She had to do it like a true warrior-princess, like a yoddha who doesn't lay down her weapon until the task is completed and the objective is achieved.

Jaan jaye toh jaye, magar himmat nahi.

She chanted her own words to herself. They proved to be a solid motivation.

Over the next couple of months, thanks to dedicated practice and her never-give-up spirit, Meera's shooting scores started to improve. She practised musketry during every free minute she was allowed in the academy's busy schedule, and soon the heavy and complicated weapons began to feel comfortable in her steady hands, like an old friend. Her shooting instructors were happy with her progress and her improvement proved to be substantial motivation for her to keep pushing the limits.

18

Meera pushed herself, training hard and getting better with every extra penalty Ustaad Manoj Kumar levied on her. She had never been someone who complained about the hardships life had dealt to her, but during the training she stopped feeling even the faintest bit sorry for herself. Self-pity was a luxury she couldn't afford, she told herself. She had no time to sit moping or crying or whining. And her progress in almost every other field kept her motivated. She knew she could do it. Things were getting better.

Then, one particular morning, when the sun was hiding behind dark clouds—the Chennai monsoon had arrived—Ustaad ordered her to do five extra laps around the obstacle-course in the training ground. She had to complete each circuit of twenty-two obstacles in fifteen minutes, a task that was usually done when the cadets weren't already exhausted after an entire session of physical training. Meera had just completed the training session with the rest of the cadets without any error or major time lapses and was in a better time category than half the class, and yet this punishment had been meted out to her. She couldn't understand the reason for this singling out, and because she was already dog-tired, Meera felt defeated that day.

As she had no option but to follow his orders, that is exactly what she did. Tears brimmed in her eyes as she took the extra five rounds of the obstacle course and finished each of them within the specified time limit, a personal record for her. By the end of the fifth circuit, her elbows were bleeding, and her right leg felt tender, but she carried on after a salute to the ustaad, who stood there, watching her like a hawk.

'He still thinks I'm not fit to be an officer and wants me to quit,' Meera said to Simran during the eleven minutes they had for lunch before classes began again. They had been up since 4 a.m., which was a habit by now, but Meera felt exhausted today—both, physically and emotionally.

'I don't think anyone in his right mind would think that,' Simran offered honestly. 'You're at the top of our course. You're decent in physical, if not the top dog. Women officers aren't yet approved to be in active combat roles anyway—so what's the problem?'

'Well, he does think that,' said Meera, sullen and dejected. What more could she do to assure him that she was fit to be an Indian Army officer?

'Nah! I feel it must be an entirely different issue,' Simran said thoughtfully. 'Maybe he doesn't like how you don't complain? Maybe he's sadistic? I mean, people are weird. It could be anything, actually.'

'Whatever,' said Meera, resolutely pushing the ustaad out her mind. She had to eat well, and she tried to spoon as much food in her mouth in the short time they had.

Time was always an issue during academy training, and Meera believed that efficient time management was another thing the cadets needed to learn during their training.

'Why aren't you eating?' Meera asked, noticing that Simran hadn't touched her food.

Simran was just pushing the food around listlessly, which was unusual. The cadets invariably ate like they had been starving for days, thanks to all the physical training and no-time issue. In fact, Meera and Simran often smuggled boiled eggs in their pockets for later, in case they didn't get to eat enough food during their short breaks. So, Simran's behaviour was very strange, Meera thought.

'I—um . . .' Simran began and stopped. She looked at Meera with an expression that made Meera stop eating, her spoon held mid-air.

'What?' Meera whispered, realizing the gravity of the situation from Simran's expression.

'I . . . I'm getting married,' Simran whispered back.

'What?' Meera was shocked.

'During the term break,' Simran shrugged like it was nothing, but her face told a different story. She looked terrified and disheartened.

'To Sunny from Chandigarh?' Meera asked in disbelief. Simran nodded.

'But you told me that you said no to your mom months ago!'

'You don't know my mom, Meera. She can emotionally blackmail me endlessly . . . she told me that my dad has given his word to Sunny's parents that I will marry him so that our businesses grow together. My dad's company is kind of tanking and he needs investment.'

'And you're the price of that investment?' Meera couldn't believe her ears.

'You don't know my mom! She didn't eat for a week and was admitted to the hospital this morning. I had to agree to this to make her eat something.' Simran was close to tears by now and looking so desperate that it made Meera's heart ache.

'And what about your training? Your life?' Meera asked. 'Do you even like Sunny?'

'It doesn't matter,' Simran said. 'Nothing matters. I'll talk to Sunny this evening and find out whether he'll allow me to continue the training.'

'*Allow* you? Is he your boss? Your owner? What has happened to you, Simran?'

'I can't let my mom die,' Simran said in a small voice.

'She won't die. This is all a drama to make you do what she wants you to do.' Meera was livid at this manipulation, this blatant disregard for Simran's own dreams and desires. 'Come on, Simran, you can't let her win!'

'She's my mother, Meera, and there's no "winning". I have to do what's right for my family,' said Simran, looking at the table instead of at Meera. 'You're lucky that you have parents who support you, Meera. You won't understand my situation,' Simran added, and then walked out of the mess hall, leaving a stunned Meera sitting at the table.

Was she lucky? While her father was still not talking to her, her mother and mother-in-law were her biggest supporters, and even her father-in-law was coming around. But she did have to lose Ranvijay to garner this support, and Meera wasn't sure if that was worth calling herself lucky. It was an emotional conundrum, but she also knew that there was nothing better than to live in the present and to have gratitude for the good things. And man, she really did have some good people in her life!

That night, Meera decided to write letters to her mother and her in-laws. She wanted them to know that she was grateful to have them around—however many the hiccups that came her way, they were always there to help her. She thought of her mother, a simple and quiet woman dressed in her trademark Rajputi poshak with the dupatta covering her head, standing up to her father to support her. She thought of her mother-in-law, dressed in her beautifully tailored Kota Doria salwar suit, encouraging Meera and her outrageous dream of joining the Indian Army, despite having lost her son to the same profession.

These two women were stronger and braver than anyone Meera had ever come across. She finished the letters and thanked her stars before sleeping that night. *Next time the ustaad makes me do extra rounds, this is what I will remember; I will remember this immense blessing.* This was the last thought Meera had that night before she succumbed to sleep.

* * *

Over the next week, Meera tried to talk some sense into Simran. Meera believed that, like the last time, Simran would handle the situation and complete her training. Leaving the training midway, after having put in so much blood, sweat, toil and tears into it seemed highly unlikely to Meera. And on top of that practical reasoning, Meera also knew about Simran's unshakable ambition to become an Indian Army officer. She shared Meera's passion and it was this that had brought them closer over the past few months.

Simran wouldn't leave the training, would she? Meera wondered every day of the week. *It would be such a waste of time, effort and potential.*

But despite her most sincere efforts, Simran quit her training by the end of that month. As Meera suspected and feared, Sunny's parents didn't want Simran to continue her training at OTA. They wanted a wife for their son who would take care of him and live a normal married life in Chandigarh. Their brand-new daughter-in-law training to be an officer in the army was out of the question.

To leave OTA mid-training, a cadet has to pay a huge amount to the army as compensation for all the money and effort it has invested in the cadet.

'In the end, it's all about investment, you see,' Simran explained to Meera as she packed her suitcase. Her future in-laws had paid the money without flinching. The whole thing reeked of tackiness to Meera. It was almost as though as soon as the price of Simran's dream had been paid, she was all theirs. Meera cried all night for her friend, and for the dream that would now die a slow and painful death. Meera scored the best points in shooting practice that day, and the instructor noted that she had shot five targets in the head, one after the other. *Maybe anger fuelled my fire today*, she thought, because she was raging at Simran's situation. It frustrated her that there was absolutely nothing she could do to help her friend.

The very next day, Ustaad punished Meera for arriving one minute late to the evening drill. As she rolled across the parade ground for three laps, the skin on her elbows was scraped raw, her knees trembled and tears flooded her eyes. She felt that the stress today was more emotional than physical. She missed Simran. But she carried on without betraying any sign of weakness, because Simran's exit from the academy was another reminder to Meera that she *had* to keep going—no matter what.

Train the mind to never give up, she kept repeating to herself.

During her last lap, a sharp stone cut the skin on her left thigh and although it was only a small cut, it started to bleed. But Meera didn't stop.

Yuddh hee toh veer ka praman hai—the lines resonated in her mind over and over again as she rolled on the ground. This was a war in its own way, and she had to prove her mettle as a warrior.

That night, as a weak and shattered Meera started to trudge tiredly back to her room after the drill ustaad had dismissed the night parade, she heard him call her name.

'Cadet Chauhan will stay behind!' his voice roared across the vast ground.

Meera walked back and stood at attention about twenty metres from him as he waited for the other cadets to leave. Standing there, Meera expected a further punishment to break her, and although she was bone tired that day—from training and from the weight of Simran's exit—she mentally prepared herself to run another lap or roll the night away around the perimeter of the grounds. She repeated her poetic motto over and over in her head, as a pep-talk to herself.

But what happened next was unexpected, to say the least.

Ustaad Manoj Kumar asked her if she was okay.

At first, Meera thought she hadn't heard him right and asked him to repeat his question; and he did.

When she nodded uncertainly, Ustaad said, 'Someone who abandons training in the middle does so because of their helplessness or weakness, but the one who is still in the academy—they don't have the luxury of helplessness or weakness.'

'*Ji*, Ustaad,' Meera responded, still flummoxed.

'After becoming an officer, a lot of similar situations will crop up that will require you to overcome your emotions and take a logical decision. You're being trained in the academy for this very reason. Never let your emotions come before your duty, Cadet Chauhan. When you become an officer, the lives of other people will also depend on your decisions. You'll need to exercise focus and patience.'

'*Ji*, ustaad,' Meera nodded. She had noticed that the ustaad said 'when' and not 'if' she became an officer. She counted that as a tiny win—a much-needed one for the kind of a day she'd just had.

'How's your shooting coming along?' he asked.

'Better, Ustaad,' she replied, not sure whether this was the time to mention yesterday's perfect result.

'Push-ups are your friend, Cadet Chauhan,' the ustaad said. Meera looked at him, perplexed. He explained, his voice still stern, 'The first requirement of shooting is arm strength. Push-ups are the best kind of musketry one can do, but very few people give it attention. Keep doing push-ups.'

'*Ji*, Ustaad,' Meera replied promptly, but she was still confused. Had all those push-up punishments been a way to strengthen her musketry? And why did the drill ustaad concern himself with her shooting anyway? This didn't make sense to Meera.

'Tomorrow morning, 4 a.m., cadet,' Ustaad said, his voice at a much lower decibel level than usual and left.

Meera didn't know what to make of it, but she decided to take the speck of positivity from this strange interaction. Maybe he felt sorry for her: everyone knew she was tight with Simran. Meera thought it was nice of the ustaad to motivate her. It made her feel happy and validated.

Smiling, she jogged back to her room, forgetting her injuries.

The next week, the academy announced a hackathon for the cadets. This was a pleasant surprise for Meera. Her ethical-hacking certification course during her engineering was something that she had taken to almost like a fish to water. She thrived in the amazing world of codes and signals. In this hackathon organized by the Military College of Telecommunication Engineering, cadets were expected to look at the digital aspects of radio frequency transmissions and try to win the challenge by solving problem statements in the radio-frequency and cyber domain. This was Meera's turf, and she participated with great gusto.

Problem-solving skills were one of Meera's strengths and as an engineer trained in hacking, it wasn't surprising that she won the hackathon by a mile. This was a good accomplishment and great motivation for Meera, but she didn't know that this win would also gain her entry into an experimental programme designed by the Indian Army and Indian government in an effort to strengthen the country's intelligence. This was currently slotted under the Directorate of Military Intelligence, and Meera was assigned extra classes under this set up, at the OTA. She would study coding and analysis from the military and national security point of view. She was already well-versed with the basics, thanks to her interest in the subject since her engineering days, but this would give her the chance to master it from a defence angle that she hadn't yet considered.

The hackathon helped her get noticed, and she was recognized as an excellent choice for army intelligence. And as the Indian Army was working hard at scaling its intelligence capacities, it was also open to women officers for the first time.

Exciting times, Meera thought happily.

Now she was required to give more hours of her day to not just her academy routine, but also to the extra classes, without compromising either. And she tried her best.

She wasn't really surprised to find the drill ustaad back to being his tough self with her. But, having spent months in the academy, small accomplishments like these, strengthened her faith in herself. She knew she could do it. She knew she was worthy. So, she carried on regardless.

A few days after the hackathon result was announced, Capt. Rana telephoned her. Ranvijay's unit officers called her frequently to check on how she was doing and to ask if she needed help in any way; and Capt. Rana called almost every week to check on his little sister's progress, and to try to help and motivate her if required. He was an NDA pass out, he knew just how tough academy life could get.

'I hear you're impressing the entire OTA cavalry with your intelligence and bratty attitude,' he teased her.

He had heard about her induction into an innovative M.I. programme after winning the hackathon, and the academy's shooting instructor was his NDA company type. But Meera, who had just finished wrapping a crepe bandage on her arm that felt injured after an extra round of push-ups given to her as a punishment by the drill ustad, was in no mood to joke.

'Not at all. No one is impressed. In fact, my drill ustaad here hates me.'

'Ustaads are tough,' Capt. Rana agreed, and remembered his own time at the NDA in Pune. 'Mine made sure I missed dinner altogether for three weeks straight because I wasn't finishing the obstacle course in the set time.'

'Just three weeks? I'd say that's still an upgrade from mine who has a special problem with just me.'

'I'm sure it's not just you, Meera.'

'I mean, it seems like that. But no complaints, he did call me to motivate me in his own strange way after my closest friend, my roommate and course mate dropped out of the training.'

'All three of them left? Together?' he asked, incredulous.

'Hahaha, very funny, Bhai-sa. They're one person,' Meera laughed despite her foul mood.

Capt. Rana laughed too.

'But on a serious note, though—a cadet dropping out after coming this far in the training?' There were just a few more months left before commissioning.

'Yeah. And it's just my luck that it was my friend,' Meera said in a matter-of-fact tone. 'At least Ustaad Manoj Kumar showed me his human side after this, so that's one positive, I guess,' she sighed.

'Havaldar Manoj is your ustaad?' Capt. Rana's voice suddenly had a sombre tone in it.

'D'you know him?' Meera asked. Even if he did, she wouldn't have been surprised. The army was a small world, as Ranvijay often said. People knew each other—it wasn't a big deal.

'I should've known,' Capt. Rana said. 'It just didn't occur to me . . .'

'Known what?' Meera asked. 'What are you talking about?'

After a few beats, he spoke.

'Meera, Havaldar Manoj Kumar is from my . . . from Ranvijay's unit. He was part of the squad the day Ranvijay was killed. In fact, he was the last one to see Ranvijay alive. He got a bullet in his body that day. One of the few who survived that attack.'

Meera couldn't believe her ears. The drill ustaad who, until very recently, seemed to hate her guts, knew Ranvijay personally? And not only knew him, but was from the same Para SF unit and had been on the mission in which Ranvijay had been murdered?

Meera remembered the first time she saw ustaad, in his crisp uniform and maroon beret. How could she have missed it! Now that she thought about it, it all made sense. He was injured during that unfortunate mission, and that was when he was posted to the academy—she had heard the stories. He was tough on Meera because, even though she didn't know him or his connection to her husband, he must have known she was Capt. Ranvijay Chauhan's wife.

Meera thought about his giving her extra rounds that used to initially break her, but had eventually built her up stronger than ever, improving not just her overall performance in physicals, but also her stamina. She remembered his taking an inexplicable interest in her shooting performance and making her do push-ups—the best form of musketry, which must have played a part in how comfortable the gun felt in her hands now, how steady and unwavering. The only reason she could think of for all the tough times she seemed to have faced with him could only be attributed to the ustaad's efforts to toughen her up, for her own good. To her, it felt like Havaldar Manoj Kumar, in his own way, was trying to do his bit to ensure that she excelled.

She felt overcome with emotion. Before hanging up the phone, Meera said to Capt. Rana: 'Bhai-sa, you'll have to tell me the complete story of that day as soon as I am commissioned. I want to know everything you know about how Ranvijay was killed . . . everything.'

19

Early the next morning, Meera considered staying back after line *tod*, the end of the session, to speak to Ustaad Manoj Kumar. She wanted to tell him that she knew who he was, and that she wanted to talk to him about Ranvijay and about that operation which had led to his murder. But after a few seconds of fidgeting, she decided against it. There was no point in this conversation; it would only make things awkward with Ustaad.

Instead, Meera decided that she would talk to him after commissioning. She was about to leave when Ustaad spoke to her.

'Cadet Chauhan, you wasted four minutes out of your fifteen-minute breakfast time. What's the matter?'

'*Kuch nahi*, Ustaad,' Meera replied. 'Sorry.' She hurried to the mess, but with a smile on her face. Incidents like these made her feel like she belonged in the army. Ranvijay might not be here any more, but his legacy would always ensure that she felt at home in the midst of these brave men and women.

Meanwhile, Havaldar Manoj Kumar looked at the cadet who had just walked away after an unnecessary apology, and as usually happened after interactions with Cadet Chauhan, sorrow cast a cloud over him. Ranvijay saab had pretty much saved his life and lost his own. And now here he was, in a strange twist of fate—training his widow to follow the same path that Ranvijay saab had walked so bravely. At a distance, Ustaad saw Cadet Meera Chauhan talking to a few other cadets from Zojila Company, and the cloud of sorrow parted to let in a shining ray of pride because he was sure that this young woman was cut out for big things. She was, after all, the widow of one of the bravest commandoes he had ever known.

* * *

Meera didn't think that the end of her academy training would come so quickly. After eleven long, laborious months, she was ready to be commissioned as an officer in the Indian Army.

On the day of the passing-out parade, Meera marched proudly with her squadron, knowing that her family members, including her father, were watching from the audience, and a dear one was hopefully watching from heaven up above.

I hope I do you proud, Meera said to Ranvijay in her mind. *As proud as I am of you.*

Her parents sat in the front row towards the left of the main stage, wiping tears of joy and pride, even her father. Her parents-in-law sat beside them, both overcome with emotions, for obvious reasons: this was their second passing-out parade; they had witnessed two young officers being commissioned across different timelines and circumstances, one of whom was no longer alive. No one can claim to escape unscathed from such a tragedy, and yet here they were, clapping enthusiastically for Meera.

Even a newlywed Simran, red *chura* on her arms, was sitting beside Meera's family, Sunny in tow, holding her camera to take a hundred pictures of Meera.

When the time came, Meera's mother and mother-in-law stepped forward to uncover the stars on her crisp uniform, both weeping softly. Meera stood to attention, overcome with pride and emotions she couldn't really register because they flooded her all at once. Her father stood by, watching, discreetly wiping his tears that threatened to spill over every so often during this morning's ceremony. Her father-in-law, on the other hand, was openly sobbing. The scene before her made her heart swell.

From Cadet Meera Chauhan she had become Lieutenant Meera Chauhan. She looked up at the heaven and for the millionth time that morning, remembered Ranvijay.

I am more proud of myself than I've ever been, she said silently to Ranvijay.

And I would still give it all up to have you back.

Just then, Ustaad Manoj Kumar came up to her. He saluted Meera, a smart, crisp salute. 'Jai Hind, saab!' Havaldar Manoj said in his booming voice. After being commissioned, Lt Meera Chauhan was now his senior, and pride shone on his face. After a few seconds of trying to decide on the best way to show her gratitude, that was as per hierarchical protocol, Meera just shook her head, stepped closer and gave him a hug. This was no time to pull rank, she had decided. She released him from that awkward embrace in a second, and then looked him in the eye.

'I know,' she said to him, tears already flowing down her face. 'I've known for a while.'

He stood uncomfortably for a second, nodded in understanding of what she had just revealed to him, and then patted her shoulder affectionately. There were tears in his eyes that he was valiantly trying to hide.

'Ranvijay saab saved my life. He was one of the toughest, most fearsome commandoes I've ever seen. If he hadn't been around, I wouldn't be here today,' he said and then continued, 'I tried to do my best with your training, saab. I tried to prepare you for the worst that is out there. Maybe this will be my service to Ranvijay saab.'

Meera nodded, finding no words to adequately respond to him. It was an emotional scene for anyone who knew the history. Everyone had tears in their eyes.

'*Ye dekho*, a Para SF commando is crying,' Meera's father-in-law joked between tears, as Naik Manoj bent down to touch his feet. 'One Chauhan saab was taken away, but now you have one more,' Ranvijay's father told Manoj Kumar, 'but wait, is she also saab? Not memsaab?'

'"Memsaab" is an officer's wife, Dad,' Meera explained. 'Women officers are also addressed as saab or sahab. Just like a woman IPS officer is addressed as saab by her team, and a woman judge is often referred to as saab. It's a gender-neutral term for us, in these fields.'

'Okay, Chauhan saab,' her mother-in-law quipped, and saluted. Everyone laughed, including Meera's father, who had been an emotional mess today.

* * *

The president of the country was the chief guest at the passing-out parade, and he congratulated the cadets on completing the training successfully.

Although the army was still not taking lady officers in combat positions as yet, Meera was satisfied. She had performed extremely well throughout the course of her training and had even excelled at physical fitness by the time she had passed out. She was commissioned to the Indian Army's Corps of Signals and, under a newly introduced programme at the academy, she was also a special, intelligence-trained officer. The Indian Army had formed a covert and experimental unit dedicated to encryption and decoding signals and it comprised officers and soldiers from both the Corps of Signals as well as the Directorate of Military Intelligence. Usually, the two operated as separate departments and came together only when required, but the Indian Defence Ministry had issued directives to explore a new set-up by joining the mighty forces of these two teams, albeit in a small, experimental structure. This team was to be based in Delhi, dedicatedly working on high importance and extremely complicated intel pieces across the board and spectrum. The success of this team would pave way for the future, and the ministry was paying special attention to this experimental department.

Meera was excited to be part of this trial, and on a personal level, she believed it would work towards making the Indian intel game stronger. She couldn't wait to join this team.

Towards the end of the ceremony, when the sun was inching towards the horizon in a bright orange hue, Capt. Rana called Meera.

'Congratulations, Lt Meera Chauhan. Onwards and upwards,' he said.

'Thank you, bhai . . . er . . . I mean, Capt. Rana,' she replied. 'Wouldn't have been here without your help, without the help of the paltan.'

'You're destined for great things, Meera; we're all just glad to be of help.'

Meera smiled wistfully, 'I wish I could've joined the same paltan.'

'There are numerous ways you can work with the paltan,' Capt. Rana offered. 'We work in this area based on timely intelligence, and the CO here has just learned that the special team, of which you're going to be a part, will also work for the same area. So, I'm sure that the opportunity to work together in whatever form or fashion will come. Army is a small world; it will happen soon by God's grace.'

'Let's hope that's true,' said Meera. There was nothing she wanted more than to be working with Ranvijay's Para SF Unit, clearing the Kashmir valley of terrorism and violence. She had always known the situation in Kashmir, but her knowledge and understanding had grown multifold after Ranvijay's passing due to her assiduous research and studies. Then, during her training, she learnt a heart-breaking yet important fact of today's world: for the preservation of peace, being prepared for war is a necessity.

And she would do her bit in the Indian Army's readiness, she promised herself. That night, after dinner, her father handed her a prettily packaged box.

'I'm sorry, beta,' he said, struggling to meet her eyes because tears kept filling his own. 'I hope you know that I'm proud of you. I'm from a different generation and I've not seen the world through your brave eyes as I ought to have. For that, I'm sorry. I didn't believe in your dreams when I should've simply trusted you. For that, I'm sorry too. But you're the bravest person I know, Meera, and you've worked hard to make your every dream come true. You've overcome the misfortune that life handed to you and here you are, smiling in an officer's uniform with stars on your shoulder. I've never been so proud and so sorry in my life. I hope you can forgive me, beta.'

He wiped his tears, and Meera fought back hers. She then hugged her father, and let her tears fall. She wept into her father's chest because after years and years of feeling let down by his rejection and opposition to each and every one of her dreams, what he had said today felt like an absolute truth. The kind of truth that was so bare and vulnerable that it gave her relief from a century of burden. Meera believed him. This was the new dawn of her relationship with her dad, one of the toughest men she knew—the one whom she had taken after. She had always known that this stubbornness, which was an integral part of her personality and had helped her overcome obstacles and hardships, came from her father.

'Thank you, Papa,' she said between sobs.

'You give them hell, beta,' her father said, patting her back. 'Those jihadis have no idea what they're up against now.'

Meera laughed in between her tears. The gift box contained a beautiful, gold-leafed, hardbound Hanuman Chalisa. It was the perfect size to be carried in a bag, and as Meera touched the book to her forehead in a respectful gesture, she decided to keep it with her at all times. She had always had faith in Bajrang Bali, even if she wasn't usually very religious. Sure, she remembered to pray in times of need and believed in a higher power up there in the heavens, but she wasn't the kind to flaunt her belief. Receiving a Hanuman Chalisa from her dad, who sometimes seemed so distant from her, touched Meera's heart deeply. With her father's open approval of her life choices now, she felt like the little girl within her was healing and happy.

What a relief! she thought with a sigh. 'Jai Bajrang Bali!' she chanted under her breath.

* * *

Meera had the next two weeks off before she reported for duty. She reached Bikaner the day after her commissioning with both sets of parents, their pride clearly evident in their tearful eyes and big smiles. In the evening, Meera's father had arranged a party in Meera's honour, and their close friends and relatives came to celebrate Meera's extraordinary success with daal baati churma and laal maas prepared by the best *halwai* in town.

It felt surreal to Meera. She had her family close, cheering for her, and yet all she could think about was Ranvijay.

His laughter.

His touch.

His warm eyes, and the rise and fall of his collarbone, which she would frequently trace with her fingertips, always ending her journey by resting her palm against the boom! boom! boom! of his heart. Although it almost always led to their reaching hungrily for each other, this wasn't a sensual gesture for Meera. It was a reverential one; one that she had never told Ranvijay about. How could she? The devotion and love she felt for Ranvijay were almost too embarrassing to admit, even to him. She didn't want to seem needy. She was a self-sufficient girl and wanted to be seen as such; but now with Ranvijay gone, she wished she had told him how the beating of his heart beneath her palm made her feel alive. How the rhythm of his heartbeat filled her with a belief that nothing was impossible.

If Ranvijay had been here with her today, Meera would've done the same thing: traced his collarbone before resting her palm on his heart to draw strength from the sheer familiarity of it.

I hope I make you proud, she whispered to Ranvijay, looking up at the stars. *But more than that, I wish I had deserved to have you with me for a longer time.*

20

The family wrapped up the party late that night, and they woke up the following morning to see Meera's face and name splashed all over an English news channel.

The media had discovered that the widow of Capt. Ranvijay Chauhan had just passed out from the Officers' Training Academy in Chennai and was now commissioned to be an officer in the Indian Army like her brave husband. This story was prime-time newsworthy and soon enough, a few other channels also started telecasting the news, using blurred video footage from Meera's passing-out parade, in which she was marching with her squadron, with some stills of her teary-eyed mother and mother-in-law affixing the stars on her uniform, and a close-up image of Meera looking up at the sky.

The headlines were dramatic.

'War Widow Ready for Revenge!' shouted the popular national English news channel that first broke the news.

'War Widow's Willpower!' announced another English news channel that apparently specialized in defence.

'Capt. Ranvijay's Revenge Plan from Heaven: Bereaved Wife Ready for Combat!' claimed another English news channel that also decided to run features on Capt. Ranvijay Chauhan along with the news about Meera's commissioning as a 'Lest-We-Forget' piece about forgotten heroes who had been brutally murdered by terrorists.

'Girls Just Wanna Have Guns: Veer Nari Proves She Can!' stated a channel that usually did fluff pieces but had decided to cover Meera for some reason.

'*Bach Ke Rahna Atank Ke Pujaruyon, Shaheed Ranvijay Ki Widhwa Aa Rahi Hai!*' warned a Hindi news channel that was also running a piece on Meera's life through animated characters.

What chaos, Meera thought, as her father-in-law told everyone to switch off the TV.

'They just want to sensationalize every damn thing; otherwise, how will they break news for twenty-four hours?' Ranvijay's dad expostulated. 'They'll keep covering this now from every absurd angle possible for the next two days.'

'Well, at least they're refreshing the public's memory about Ranvijay's murder,' Meera's mother-in-law noted. 'Public memory is short—we never remember our heroes.'

Which was true, Meera realized. India was constantly at war in Kashmir, and while the country bled equally upon every soldier and civilian's death at the hands of terror, it was impossible to remember everyone, every hero. Ranvijay's murder had been extensively covered at the time of his death, but other and more current news items had replaced it within a matter of days, as is the norm. That was to be expected, she thought; there were a lot of things happening in the world that needed the public's attention.

But today, she wondered if the sacrifices meant the same even if no one remembered it.

She wondered if the same heroes, who had valiantly fought for a cause bigger than themselves, would do the same knowing that they would be forgotten with time . . .

Lying awake in her bed that night, Meera realized that even though she was an army officer now, it still wasn't easy for her to fully comprehend the true meaning of being a hero. What made a soldier a hero? Was it the elevated danger involved in the job? In that case, wasn't every soldier a hero? They must be. And what about selflessness and sacrifice? Was it the dedication to one's duty or was it valuing one's teammates' lives more than your own?

What was it that drove heroes to place duty for nation above everything else, including their loved ones, their personal dreams and their own lives, Meera wondered.

What was it that motivated Ranvijay that day to fight the most basic urge for survival and remain at the spot, trying to save his squad? What was it that kept Ranvijay from being selfish for one moment?

Meera knew the answer lay somewhere in the middle of all of these questions, and that it could be different for each individual.

Meera didn't have her own answer in that moment, but something in her gut told her that she would find out very soon.

The next morning, the family found, to their pleasant surprise, that not only was there no news coverage about Meera on any channel, but all news pertaining to her and her recent commissioning into the Indian Army seemed to have been magically erased from everywhere online. Everything on her had vanished overnight. The videos that the news channels usually relayed on their websites and YouTube channels, the text features and articles posted just yesterday— everything was gone!

* * *

'Khayyam Anwar?' Meera whispered in a tiny voice that was barely audible on the phone. She had called Capt. Rana to talk about the news channels' coverage, but also, and more importantly, she wanted to now hear the full account of Ranvijay's murder. She hadn't had the clearance to some of the information as a civilian and was hoping Capt. Rana would be able to tell her the whole story now that she was an Indian Army officer like him, and like Ranvijay had been.

And Capt. Rana had told her the truth. He had always felt that Meera deserved to know. The truth could either be liberating or a burden but, he believed, the truth enabled human beings to take suitable action based on informed decisions.

As expected, Meera knew who Khayyam Anwar was. She had been obsessed with the unrest in Kashmir ever since Ranvijay's passing and had studied the different aspects of the issue. She knew a great deal about the various terror organizations that were active in the region, about the fringe separatist groups that aided anti-India sentiments and of course, she knew the commander-in-chief of Lashkar.

'Ranvijay told me about the unnerving phone conversation he'd had with someone whose identity had been unknown at the time, after his squad had eliminated a few terrorists carrying ammunition, including a very young youth,' Meera recounted. 'I remember it clearly, because it sounded an alarm bell in my head even then.'

'Ranvijay wasn't happy about the kid's death,' Capt. Rana admitted. 'He felt that what happened hadn't been right and wanted to report it as an intelligence error, but I pacified him over dinner that night. To me, the lad was collateral damage. I didn't think about it again, to be honest. But he did; I could tell. Ranvijay was haunted by the killing of that kid because, even though he had no qualms about getting rid of terrorists with the blood of innocent Indian citizens on their hands, he thought there was a chance that this kid had only been in the wrong place at the wrong time. Ranvijay believed that there was a chance he was innocent.'

'But he wasn't,' Meera observed. 'He was with the terrorists, hiding deep inside a forest. There is no way he was there accidentally.'

'I think so too. In wars like this, a soldier needs to view a situation in black-and-white, right or wrong, enemy or friend, and react in the moment. More often than not, we only have a few measly seconds to make a snap decision and issue orders during an active mission. So, we do what we're taught to do: eliminate danger and minimize damage. But Ranvijay was cut from a different cloth and while he knew that, in that moment, it had been the right thing to do, he wondered if there could've been a way to capture the kid, instead of killing him,' said Capt. Rana.

'I cannot believe this. The media reported that what had happened to Ranvijay was premeditated murder, but I never imagined that the entire thing was an elaborate ruse to lure him. It's giving me the chills,' Meera admitted.

'And what haunts me, Meera,' Capt. Rana said in a voice heavy with regret, 'is the fact that the CO had originally assigned Ranvijay's final mission to me.'

'Oh!' Meera gasped. Her mind awhirl at the alternative ending . . . thinking about what could've been, instead of what had been.

'Yes. No one knows except the CO and me. And Ranvijay, of course,' he said, his voice suddenly sounding so far away. 'And now, I'm telling you.'

Meera was stunned. Both, by the information and by the fact that Capt. Rana had kept this crucial information from her for so long. She didn't know what to think or what to make of it.

'It was my birthday that day. I had applied for leave, but it got cancelled at the last moment and Sameera was so mad at me. She had planned an entire party for me, had booked a fancy rooftop hotel and had sent out invitations. She wasn't happy about having to cancel all that and she was sad about not being with me on yet another milestone.'

'Life of a fauji girlfriend-slash-wife,' Meera said in a matter-of-fact tone. She knew what it felt like to the person on the other side; she had been that person for a long time, dealing with cancelled plans and being alone on important days.

'Yeah . . . but also, she was going to officially propose to me that day, in front of all our friends and family. Everyone, except me, knew; it was meant to be a surprise for me,' Capt. Rana said. He sounded sad. 'She told me right after I was assigned the mission and at the time it made me feel guilty and ashamed for not being there for the people whom I loved and who loved me. It was a weak moment for me. And when Ranvijay learnt about this, he felt that I should be at the base, talking to her and resolving things, instead of setting off on a mission. He suggested that I stayed back, and he be assigned to the mission instead, and . . . I agreed.'

Meera could almost feel the waves of guilt and regret emanating through the phone.

'I agreed and the CO agreed. He said he hadn't planned on assigning it to me in the first place because it was my birthday. The reason he had given it to me instead of Ranvijay, even though it was Ranvijay's territory—the area was divided into parts and each of us were familiar with the terrain assigned to us—was that he thought I could use a distraction from my personal drama.'

'But Ranvijay took it back from me, convincing the CO that I needed to sort things out with my girlfriend, and this was his territory anyway. And off he went.'

'I don't think the weight of my regret will ever let me breathe normally again, Meera,' Capt. Rana continued. 'It should've been me. I should've been the one who had died that day, not Ranvijay. Not a day goes by when I don't run the series of events of that day over and over in my head, playing out other scenarios in which he didn't die the death that was meant for me.'

Meera took all of it in—the heavy information, the possibility of an alternative scenario in which Ranvijay was alive; the pain in Capt. Rana's voice; the dark cloud of grief looming over both of them in this moment—and let it all wash over her.

'But,' she began after a long pause, 'we know that Khayyam was after Ranvijay to take revenge for his brother Junaid's death, Capt. Rana. He had masterminded the entire ruse for Ranvijay—and God knows how many times he had tried before or how many times he would have tried later to level his personal score with Ranvijay,' Meera continued. 'You have to accept that Khayyam would've settled it with Ranvijay one way or the other. Even if you had gone on that mission that day, even if it had been you who had been killed that day instead of Ranvijay, Khayyam would've still gone after Ranvijay. And because we had no inkling of his plan, Ranvijay would've been murdered regardless. And we'd have lost both him and you, Bhai-sa.'

'I understand what you're saying, but I still can't shake the guilt. Believe me, I've tried. It's a constant part of me now; and everything I've done since that day, every mission I undertake, I go in wanting to avenge Ranvijay— or die trying.'

'Capt. Rana, I, too, want to take my revenge on Khayyam and on every terrorist who has spilled Indian blood. That is my biggest dream, my every prayer. And I hope we get to avenge Ranvijay—*together*,' Meera said, finding a strength of character that often eluded even the most noble of human beings in times like this. 'But both of us know that it might remain a pipedream. Khayyam is so elusive that no one has seen or heard directly from him in years on our intelligence networks. He makes no public appearances and there are no recent pictures of him or any evidence of his presence in the valley or even in POK, as far as I've been able to track. But you're doing more than your bit, and I'll do mine to keep this country safe. And I want you to remember that, while the grief of his death will always be with the ones who loved him, Ranvijay's murder is not your cross to carry. It wasn't your fault.'

'I picked up his body parts, Meera,' Capt. Rana choked on the words. It was clear to Meera that this was the first time this tough commando was discussing what he had gone through on that fateful day with another living soul. 'The sight is imprinted on my brain.'

There were a few long moments of silence, until Meera finally said, 'Thank you for sharing this with me, Capt. Rana.' She meant it.

She was shocked and in pain to hear the full story of how Ranvijay had been ruthlessly targeted, and she could only imagine how much he must've suffered before he finally died: it sent shock waves across her heart. But now she knew the truth, and information was power. She could decide her next actions based on what she knew now. She felt both burdened by a fresh wave of grief and empowered by the truth. It was a strange place to be.

Something in Meera wanted to comfort Capt. Rana, the brother who had been a pillar of strength to her over the years. It was her turn to provide the strength he needed.

'The Indian Army is much stronger in the technology we use now, and it's being strengthened every day. We're far superior in terms of skill sets as well, and I'm sure we'll get justice soon. Until then, let's prepare ourselves and be ready,' she told him. 'And I hope you'll believe me when I say, Ranvijay would hate to see you blame yourself for this. It wasn't your fault.'

Capt. Rana didn't respond, but she hoped her words had made him feel a bit better.

21

The two weeks of leave passed quickly for Meera in Bikaner.

Finally, on the last day, when she was all packed and leaving Ranvijay's parental home—she preferred to live here now; with all her memories of Ranvijay, this was her home—Ranvijay's mother did the traditional *aarti* for good luck and safety. This was a tradition their families followed and Meera was happy to stand there as her mother-in-law performed the quick ritual to ward off the evil eye. And then, Meera's father-in-law stepped forward and put a long red *teeka* on her head—something that was reserved for male members of the family. As he put some raw rice on top of the teeka, he said to an awestricken Meera, '*Tum hamara baccha ho*, Meera beta. You've made us proud and you'll continue to make us proud. I just know it! There's no one else who deserves this *jeet ka tilak* more than you.'

Meera's eyes prickled with tears.

He then handed her a thin file folder that had the popular *balidan* emblem printed on top, along with the sign of Ranvijay's Para SF Unit. The file had a gold ribbon around it and was clearly meant as a gift for her. Looking at her father-in-law with curiosity, Meera untied the ribbon. She opened the folder and stood staring at the contents for a long time, tears silently streaming down her face.

Inside, on a piece of paper, which looked like it had been held, read and folded several times, was Piyush Mishra's heroic and inspiring poem 'Aarambh Hai Prachand', written in a handwriting Meera recognized as her father-in-law's.

'I wrote this poem down for him the first time he left for NDA. I wrote it on the night before, after he had gone to sleep,' Ranvijay's father explained. 'I thought that life in NDA, and life in the army would be tough, so I wanted him to have something personal to stay motivated and to never lose faith, or his sense of *karm* and *dharm*. And I'm not creative, so I copied one of my favourite Hindi poems for Ranvijay.'

Meera held the piece of paper against her heart.

'I didn't see it after that, and I forgot about it over time. But when Ranvijay's unit sent his stuff home, I found it amongst a pile of his books. Looks like he had saved it along with this file,' he said, pride in his voice. 'Maybe he even read it a few times ...'

'He loved this poem, Papa,' Meera said to him. 'It kept him motivated. He would recite lines from it often, even to encourage me.'

'It's yours now. May it motivate you on your path,' he said lovingly, and she nodded.

'Stay safe, beta,' Ranvijay's mother said now. 'And give those terrorists hell.'

Just then, Meera's parents arrived. They were all going together to see Meera off at the railway station. Meera replaced the handwritten poem in its folder and tucked it safely in her backpack.

Aarambh Hai Prachand, she said to herself—this was indeed the start of her new life.

And that is how she bid her goodbye to leave for Delhi and report for duty.

***

It had been a few weeks since Meera had joined duty and started working alongside a team of fellow officers on decoding and encrypting signals and messages picked up by various intelligence agencies on the ground. She was living in a guest room near Gopinath Market in Delhi Cantt and was hoping to be allotted a single officer's accommodation soon, although she had been told that it often took ages to get accommodation in Delhi.

These were early days yet and there was a lot to learn, but Meera was already enjoying her work. She was assigned to a special task of mapping fragments of signals snagged by the Indian Government intelligence to other messages with similar indicators. Meera threw herself wholeheartedly into it and worked hard.

One day, she received a call from Lt Col Iyer, Ranvijay's second-in-command. He was calling to congratulate her on passing out and on the special posting. He had been on a UN mission for the past few months, which was why he hadn't been able to call earlier. He asked her about her set-up, her role and offered to help in any way possible. She

learnt that Lt Col Iyer had cleared the board and was all set
to take over the command of Ranvijay's unit in less than a
month. The news made her happy: good people deserved
to succeed in life.

Lt Col Iyer then told her that the defence ministry had
been responsible for blacking out media coverage of her
joining the army.

'Ranvijay was targeted, ma'am. Terrorism being
common in those parts of our country, targeting of army
convoys and vehicles is quite a frequent occurrence. But
a meticulously planned assault aimed at one particular
individual has never been heard of before, not in all my
extensive years of service at least,' he explained. 'Ranvijay
was taken away from us, but even in his absence, the Indian
Army and ministry believe in taking care of our families and
covering all possible grounds where the safety of families is
concerned. That is why the news about you was censored.'

'D'you think he'll come after me if he knew about me?'

'Who are you referring to, ma'am?' Lt Col Iyer asked.
His voice seemed normal, but Meera could imagine his
surprise. As far as he was concerned, Meera wasn't supposed
to know the details.

'The same terrorist who targeted Ranvijay,' she deflected.
Now was not the time to pick this battle. 'I followed the
news coverage around Ranvijay's incident, sir. I've seen
the speculations that a powerful terrorist was gunning for
Ranvijay to avenge some terrorist whom Ranvijay and his
squad had eliminated.'

'Well, we don't know,' he said, seeming to have bought
her reasoning. 'But then again, we didn't know he was
planning the attack on Ranvijay either, did we? Better to
be safe.'

'But we will know now, sir,' said Meera. 'We have much superior tech now compared to what I know we had back then. The upgrade in recent years has been massive, and I can personally assure you that if the same terrorists were to plan another offensive, we'll definitely know.'

'Good to know that, ma'am,' he said. 'Take care and hope to see you soon. And oh yes, welcome to the army.'

In the next couple of months, Capt. Rana picked up the next rank as well, and was now Major Vikram Rana. A mere six hours after his pipping ceremony, he eliminated two terrorists during an encounter in the Bandipore district of Kashmir. Meera contacted one of her OTA course-mates posted in the same area as Maj. Rana was, and arranged to send him a cake with 'Major Bhai Swag' written in icing.

* * *

October 2017

Meera has been working long enough on encrypted, signal-based intelligence now to be able to recognize a pattern and she was sure that what she was seeing on her screen was one.

She called her seniors to inform them immediately.

Over the past few months, the nature of terror attacks in the Kashmir valley had changed. Instead of haphazard explosions or aiming for army placements or even army convoys, the recent terror attacks seemed to be focused on inflicting maximum civilian damage. This indicated an emergence of a new and advanced level of warfare, where no terror organization claimed responsibility for the attack.

This was known as Black Ops, and it gave terror-funding states and countries a way out to escape global pressure. If terror attacks weren't claimed or attributed to anyone, how could anyone be blamed? It was a clever tactic, one that reeked of a larger strategic coherence and convergence in terror groups that were active in Kashmir. There was something that was bringing them all together.

The pattern that Meera had uncovered recently reinforced this theory.

While decoding signals captured over the past few weeks, she found that some seemingly unrelated and even irrelevant pieces of communication carried a similar signature. This meant that they were emerging from the same source. But what was interesting—or alarming—was that their intended receivers were meant to be across the country, and across any one organization.

Someone was not only uniting the various terror groups, but also held the power to guide them singlehandedly. This was massive news.

As Meera continued to display exceptional talent and determination as part of the ambitious Signals-and-M.I. combined intelligence team, there were bigger, more audacious things being planned for her.

Indian Army's intelligence had grown stronger over the years and with the government's focus on technology, the teams were equipped with the latest and most advanced tools. There could be no strategy without reliable intelligence and no winning without strategy—and with the ministry's focus on intelligence, Meera believed that they were on the winning side.

* * *

December 2019

Meera sat at the edge of her bed in her room in Delhi, holding her Movement Order. She had received a call just an hour ago. Meera had to report to Col Iyer within the next twenty-four hours, at an Indian Army establishment in the hills of Kupwara district. She was being attached to Ranvijay's Para SF unit for the mission that was aimed at taking down Khayyam Anwar and six other Lashkar leaders. Her intel had put the wheels in motion for this mission and she had just discovered that she was going to play a crucial part in it. This was everything she could've ever dreamed of but, in that moment, she sat, frozen.

She was going to the same place where Ranvijay had been murdered. She was finally going to get her revenge.

There was a lot to do in very little time, but she allowed herself a few minutes of silence.

As if in a trance, she went to the shelf in the corner of her room where she kept a few books. She pulled out the old file with the Balidan badge and the Para SF unit's symbol on its cover. She opened it and tenderly ran her fingers over the piece of paper, like she was afraid to inadvertently damage the old document. She had read it multiple times over the course of her service and it had always imbued her with instant courage.

She started to read the poem out loud, chanting it like a song, in a voice so soft only she could hear it. As she sang it, she felt the words fill her with something more than just courage . . . this time, the poem gave her faith.

Maut annt hai nahi | Toh maut se bhi kyoun darein

(Death is not the end | Then why should we fear death?)

Meera sat motionless, the paper still in her hand. She had often wondered about the qualities that separated heroes from regular people. In this monumental moment, she thought about the concept of heroes again ...

What was that enigmatic realm in a hero's mind in which basic survival instinct was overshadowed by the willingness to sacrifice one's life for a purpose higher than self? What purpose was deemed higher than survival? And what were the things worthy of dying for? These were questions that often plagued her, and today they came to mind again.

Ever since the previous whirlwind of a week when this extraordinary intel came to light and then, this mission, she had been in an internal turmoil. She thirsted for a revenge meted out with her own hands and wanted to be the one who killed Khayyam. She wanted payback. At the same time, her mind kept going back to heroism, what it took to be a hero and whether she had it in her. Were the two connected? She didn't know yet.

Perhaps this mission would give her the answers she sought. Maybe getting payback for what she had suffered at the hands of Khayyam Anwar would lift the fog. And maybe, just maybe, she would find the hero within herself when she eliminated her husband's murderer. And as Ranvijay's father had said to her over the phone a few years ago, although she still struggled to find it, maybe this mission would be the *aarambh* (beginning) of her heroism.

* * *

It was a crisp winter morning in Kashmir and Meera was standing outside her guest room at the transit camp, taking in the stunning white landscape. The air was cold and unforgiving. She had been in the transit camp for only a few hours, without the luxury to experience the beauty of the state known as heaven on earth, but Meera already knew that every word of praise Ranvijay had said about the beauty of Kashmir was true. The view was serene and almost like a piece of poetry that moved her heart. If one didn't know about the terrors faced by this state on a cruelly regular basis, it would be easy to see romance everywhere you looked.

I wish you were here with me, Ranvijay, Meera thought.

She was waiting to set out for the unit location, which was a few hours ahead of this transit camp. She would have been on the road by now along with her team of two radio-operator soldiers, but Maj. Rana had called and had asked her to wait for him. He had been stationed in Sopor before being deployed for this mission. Meera was aware that Maj. Rana was leading the mission, along with a squad that consisted of some of the most lethal Para SF commandoes of the unit.

'Let's travel together in one convoy,' he had said. 'I need to speak to you before this operation begins.'

Meera guessed that Maj. Rana had probably wanted to utilize the travel time to bring her and her team—the only three people on this mission with no active combat experience—up to speed with their plan of action and explain how this was going to work to ensure the success of the mission. She had agreed to wait for him.

In about an hour, Maj. Rana was there. Although Meera was eager to leave for their common destination right away, Maj. Rana asked her to follow him into the guest room.

'Meera, I need to speak to you before this begins,' Maj. Rana said the moment they were both seated on the wooden sofas inside the guest room.

'Sir, you don't have to worry. Even if I may seem like the weakest link right now, I'm fully prepared to give it my best. I know I have no combat or CI/CT experience, but I can assure you that I am capable. I'll do my utmost and ensure I'll—'

'Meera, stop,' Maj. Rana interrupted her, shaking his head. This is when Meera noticed the dark shadow over his face. 'It's not . . . it's not about your capability or inexperience.'

Meera looked at him questioningly. Maj. Rana squared his shoulders as if steeling himself for a difficult task: 'I want to make a promise to you, today,' he said raggedly, 'if my God is on my side tomorrow, I'll ensure that it's your bullet that kills Khayyam. It'll be the day you get your revenge, Meera. And I'll do everything in my power to get you your payback.'

He said it with such naked sincerity that it made Meera's heart ache. She was taken aback by his frankness and overwhelmed by the sudden surge of her emotions. She understood his need for privacy to take her into his confidence like this. The promise to give her a shot at exacting her vengeance was probably unofficial, she realized, and she was rendered speechless at the raw emotion in Rana's face. She just gaped at him.

'Meera?'

'Sir,' Meera quickly gathered herself.

'I'll do everything in my power. He'll be your kill. You have my word,' he reiterated, his eyes looked steely with the palpable hunger Meera knew had festered in him ever since Ranvijay was murdered.

'Roger, sir. It's an honour to be on this mission under your lead,' Meera said after a pause.

'It's time for payback,' Maj. Rana said. The resolve in his voice was rock solid. 'God willing, the entire paltan will be able to sleep at night after tomorrow.'

Meera's heart ached all the more now. She felt Maj. Rana's pain—of course she did. She wanted what he wanted, probably more. In this moment, Meera had absolute clarity after hours of restlessness. It was indeed time for payback for the entire paltan, and it was time for her to discover what heroism meant to her.

'Yes, sir,' she said.

Maj. Rana nodded and got up to leave. 'Let's get going. We have a bastard to kill,'

Their convoy moved towards the unit's location, where Col Iyer was waiting for them.

22

Meera gripped her gun tightly in both hands and moved quickly and stealthily along with the rest of the squad. They had to keep their movement absolutely quiet, especially around Keran, the small village which they had to skirt around to reach their location above the hill.

As soon as the ascent began, the thick forest provided perfect cover to the team, and they picked up their pace. The wind began to howl through the trees and Meera felt Nature was on their side, cheering them on. Meera was towards the end of the squad and as the climb grew steeper, she looked ahead and spotted the sniper team change their stance to alert positions with their rifles ready for action. *We must be close*, Meera thought. Her team walked beside her, carrying their radio equipment. Even as a trained soldier, and now part of a Para SF operation, the experience felt surreal for Meera. Ranvijay had told her many times about the indomitable courage and exemplary valour that distinguished them from the rest, and today Meera felt it all around her. Combat uniforms, most of the faces streaked with black paint as part of camouflage and a wide range of weapons for any and all possibilities; the sight made her feel privileged to be there, in that moment. Ranvijay was right: there was the formidable Indian Army with all its skillsets and arms and then, there was the Para SF—a cut above the rest.

Filled with anticipation and admiration, underpinned by a sliver of nervous energy, Meera kept pace with the rest of the team.

They arrived at the location within the next hour, and Meera took up her designated position along with her radio operators. As her team silently rigged their equipment at the edge of the encampment, in a spinney of thick trees, Meera did a quick visual sweep of her surroundings. She could see a few scattered huts and while the main house, where the meeting was expected to happen, was out of her sight, she could see the curve of the river Kishenganga clearly. As part of the outermost cordon, the farthest from their target, she knew they were rendered almost invisible to the naked eye by the lush foliage around them. The commando leading the third team, the outer cordon, radioed in confirmation of their position to Maj. Rana.

Team 3 waited with bated breath for the other two teams to confirm their positions as well. This was a crucial part of the plan—each team had to confirm that they were in their allocated positions before the operation could begin.

The forest was filled with bird calls, rustling leaves and creaking branches. It was wet, and cold—there was about two feet of snow on the ground. Lying prone, propped on her elbows in snow mixed with mud and fallen leaves, Meera reached for her personal radio secured by her belt on the right side of her waist, and pressed the switch. Within forty seconds, Meera heard Havaldar Siddhu whisper, 'Team 2. All in position.'

Now Team 1, the assault-and-the-fire-support teams will be moving into position, Meera thought. Within thirty seconds, Maj. Rana's voice, low and steady, came through the radio device. 'Team 1. All in position.'

The stage was set. Meera felt goosebumps prickle at the back of her neck.

Ahead of Meera and the outer cordon, Maj. Rana crouched behind the kuccha wall of an uninhabited hut and took out his night-vision binoculars. The entire area looked deserted with no human in sight. Most of the huts were empty and seemed abandoned, just as they had expected. Shepherds who lived here seasonally, usually vacated this area at the start of winter and didn't return until mid-April.

'Accessing target,' he said on the radio, in a low voice, holding the binoculars to his eyes. Moving his viewfinder towards the target location—a bigger hut with faint lights escaping through the window—Maj. Rana scanned for signs of human presence. The lights were a dead giveaway but they had to confirm the presence of terrorists before launching their assault. Within a few seconds, he spotted two of the terrorists whom Meera's intelligence had identified. One was sitting on the floor with his back against the wall and the other was standing, folding what looked like a shawl. And then a third person walked in and sat down beside the first man. All three of them were wearing cloak-like pherans.

Three out of the seven terrorists about whom they had information were present at the location—this was confirmation enough to launch into action. They were ready to go. Maj. Rana took a deep breath and gave the go-ahead signal.

'Target identified,' he said over the radio. 'Three out of seven.'

Meera knew that this was just a confirmation from a distance and the rest of the terrorists could be inside the house, but she nonetheless sent up a silent prayer: *Please let Khayyam be there, please!*

Maj. Rana's voice floated over the radio again: 'Operation Payback—ready for action. Team 1, go at three.'

It was time for payback, indeed. In that moment, every commando in the squad surrounding the target from all sides counted to three in their heads together with Maj. Rana, who spoke on the radio in a voice so low yet steady that it felt eerie to Meera as she listened through her device.

'Three,' said Maj, Rana. The wind picked up pace. 'Two.'

Meera took a sharp breath, her heart in her mouth— she felt more alive than ever.

'One.'

* * *

In the next second, the operation was underway. The assault team broke down the wooden door and strategically threw grenades inside, as part of the room-intervention drill. Grenades blasted and the sound reverberated through the forest. The team of commandoes then entered the house and opened fire.

'Escape attempt, west window!' one of the assault-team commandoes relayed the radio message amidst the firing.

The inner cordon focused on the window and Havaldar Siddhu's sniper took out the escaping terrorist before he was even fully out of the window.

In the outer cordon, Meera and her team were alert, ready to spring into action at the first sign of anyone escaping into their area. Meera was constantly checking on the equipment, tuning it to perfection to monitor the frequencies. There were no unidentified signals emanating from the area so far.

In a few minutes, the firing stopped and the area fell silent—the birds had also fled the trees in the area. The silence after the hellfire sounded deafening to Meera, as her stomach roiled in anticipation of news from the assault team.

And then Maj. Rana's voice came from the radio set: 'Nine eliminated.'

Meera caught her breath. *Nine?*

'Six as identified.' Which meant six of the nine eliminated were those identified from the intelligence report. 'Three unidentified,' Maj. Rana conveyed.

'Khayyam?' Meera couldn't stop herself. She had to know. The radio set was silent for a tense moment, and then she heard Maj Rana's voice.

'Khayyam negative.'

'Negative?' Meera exclaimed.

'Negative,' Maj Rana confirmed. 'Not here. Wasn't here.'

This meant that Khayyam hadn't been in the house when the assault team of commandoes broke in. *But how is that possible?* Meera thought. *The purpose of this meeting was to align strategy with him—this group wouldn't have assembled here in the first place if Khayyam wasn't going to be present.*

'He has to be here,' she said, almost to herself.

'He isn't,' Maj. Rana's voice came from the device. 'Maybe he didn't turn up.'

And with this, he ordered the teams to 'wait and watch'—a standard procedure in situations like these, in which the squad could still be susceptible to terrorists lurking around or any undetonated explosives in the area. The teams would now lie low and stay alert, assessing the situation and eliminating all possible chances of danger, before moving to the next step—site clearance. Everyone took their designated places and observed 'wait and watch'.

But not Meera. She was busy fiddling with the device, hoping to catch a signal, any sign that would convince the team that Khayyam was indeed here and would escape if they didn't try to capture him.

She slipped on her headset and twiddled the controls on her receivers. She did it again. And again.

Nothing. The frequency she was monitoring wasn't very strong and had occasional blank spots, but she hoped to pick up something, anything! Desperate for a signal, she hauled the device a few metres to her right, towards the river.

'Saab,' one of the operators said to her; but she had her headset on, and she continued moving in the direction where there was a lighter tree cover, hoping the scantier foliage would help improve the strength of the signal.

A feeling of despair crept up her body. Angry tears flooded her eyes. *All this for nothing? Operation Payback and where is the payback?*

She tuned the device once more. Over the static, she suddenly heard a faint voice. She froze and pressed the headset closer to her ears in an attempt to hear more clearly.

'Indian Army is here,' came the voice, very faint. '... ambush ... *shahadat* ... safe.' She could only hear sporadic segments of what was being said, but some words stood out.

Standing still, her hands pressing the headset to her ears, Meera shut her eyes and focused only on the voice on the radio. Everything else, all the other sounds of the world, were tuned out.

After a few beats, the voice came again.

'We weren't inside, Insha'Allah. Heading northwest on foot, should meet the rescue troop in twenty to twenty-five minutes.'

There was no time to think. In a frenzy of rage, Meera threw the headset beside the radio receiver equipment which she had dragged almost fifty metres away from its original spot, and ran, clutching her AK-47 towards what she suspected was the location. Northwest of the establishment would lead to POK if one were able to ford the river.

'Northwest,' she yelled at the two operators from her team as she ran. 'Khayyam,' she shouted, hoping they would get the context. She had no time to explain. Khayyam was escaping and no one in the squad even knew he was there!

Moving as quickly as she could with the combined weight of the weapon and her combat suit; she continued to scan the area for any movement ahead of her. But the forest seemed deserted, the foliage denser around her now, and quieter. She kept running. About two hundred metres in and there was still no sign of any movement. Meera stopped and looked around. The quiet forest stayed motionless; not a leaf rustled.

Khayyam has managed to escape, she thought, hot tears of rage and defeat streaming down her face. *And no one in the squad even knew he was here. He had evaded them yet again!*

She looked up at the sky through the canopy of the tall trees and wiped away her tears. She knew she had failed. She had failed the squad; she had failed Ranvijay. Now sobbing uncontrollably with rage, she squeezed her eyes shut and screamed at the sky in anguish, 'Khayyyyaaaam!'

Her voice echoed around the forest and she heard it come back to her. She opened her eyes and felt the sting of tears.

Just then, the wooden butt of a heavy assault rifle bludgeoned the back of her head. Meera fell to the ground, face first.

* * *

The shooting pain in her head felt like she had been shot, but she wasn't. The blunt-force trauma made her vision blurry as she attempted to get back on her feet, clutching her AK-47. But before she could get up, a tall figure loomed over her and flipped her over with his boot. In a swift movement that took half a second, Meera took out a knife from her pocket and stabbed at him. The blade slashed his leg but didn't get lodged in it as she had hoped, because someone grabbed her from behind simultaneously. She felt a hefty kick in her back and she doubled over in pain. A third man appeared now and wrested her AK-47 from her.

Grimacing in pain, Meera assessed the situation—she was about two hundred metres from her original location;

three terrorists surrounded her at that moment; and her main weapon had been taken away. To make matters worse, her vision was still blurred. She looked up to see the person whose boot had flipped her over. In an olive-green combat jacket over a black pheran, face obscured by a woollen scarf, his head cocked to one side as his eyes assessed her, the man said mockingly, 'Indian Army has started sending girls to fight us now? I feel insulted.' He guffawed.

In that moment, Meera instinctively knew that this was Khayyam. There was no proof, his face was hidden, but she just knew. Fresh rage filled her and she aggressively attempted to break free of the man who held her arms in an iron grip behind her, and had to be satisfied with kicking Khayyam's shin where she had slashed him.

At this, Khayyam bent down to stare into her face in a threatening way and gripped her face tightly, 'Your army hurt my feelings by sending a girl,' he said to her, 'and you injured my leg. This is not a good day, officer—what's your name?' he paused to look at her name tag. His eyes found hers again, but there was a menacing amusement in them now. Slowly, he unwrapped the scarf from around his face.

'Lt Meera Chauhan,' he murmured, tossing his scarf to the terrorist beside him, signalling to him to tie her hands behind her. The man immediately obeyed.

'Lt Meera Chauhan,' he repeated her name as if he were trying to place it, his eyes on her face. His eyes glinted as he smiled. He had made the connection.

'Capt. Ranvijay Chauhan,' he said. 'Lt Meera Chauhan. Looks like the Chauhan family is destined to die by my hand.'

The third terrorist had bound her wrists so tightly together that she felt the blood flow to her hands had stopped. The two terrorists moved to stand beside Khayyam, facing her now. Meera's AK-47 was casually slung across the back of one of Khayyam's goons.

Meera slumped backwards, crying out in pain and Khayyam laughed. What he didn't notice was that, with this small movement, Meera was able to push the button of her radio transmitter.

* * *

Back at the base of operations, Maj. Rana sprang into action at the sound of voices coming from Meera's transmitter. Just a few minutes ago, he had arrived at the spot from where Meera had rushed into the forest, giving a direction and saying Khayyam's name as she ran. The leader of the outer cordon had alerted him. From what the operators had said, he understood that Meera must have intercepted a signal and located Khayyam. Just then, he heard voices coming through the receiving device on Meera's set.

He didn't know how many terrorists were there, and he didn't want to lose time—Meera's life was at stake! He ran in the direction she had taken, listening intently to the radio messages via his headset.

'*Janab*,' one of the terrorists said, 'we should get going. Should I shoot her?'

Meera glared at Khayyam, unflinching, naked hatred and rage on her face.

'I'd love to gouge out your eyes as well, little girl,' Khayyam said to Meera, 'but I'm short on time, thanks to your army. And if I kill you, who'll narrate horror stories about us to the Indian Army?'

About a hundred metres away now, Maj. Rana heard this on his headset and quickened his pace, scanning the area and trying to spot them.

'Tell them that Kashmir will see Diwali every month now—*bade phatake wali* Diwali,' he smiled.

'Leave her alive,' he ordered the terrorist who had suggested killing her, 'but break her leg.'

In a second, the two men hauled her upright. One held her steady and the other grabbed her right leg, yanked it to a side and kicked it hard from behind her. Meera screamed in agony as she felt her bone crack with the impact. With one more kick to her back, the terrorist shoved her to her side, her hands still tied behind her and got up.

'Chalo,' said Khayyam. 'We've wasted six minutes here; we need to hurry.'

And with that, the three terrorists walked away swiftly. The confidence with which they moved through the woods demonstrated how well they knew the terrain. Meera struggled to free her hands, the pain in her right leg almost blinding her.

Just then, Maj. Rana appeared by her side. Everything from then onwards happened in a flash.

Three commandoes from about forty metres behind Maj. Rana gave him cover fire. Maj. Rana propped up Meera in a sitting position and cut the scarf binding her hands. Khayyam and his two henchmen realized the commandoes were close at their heels and fired at them as they plunged deeper into the undergrowth.

'Sir,' Meera said to Maj. Rana, her voice quavering with pain and the high decibel anticipation of the moment.

'Yes, you will kill him today,' Maj. Rana said.

Now that her hands were free, Meera retrieved the backup pistol stowed in the holster around her ankle and aimed at the fleeing terrorists.

'Khayyam's head, Meera,' Maj. Rana said to her. 'Take the shot.' His gun was also pointed in that direction, Meera noticed. But he wasn't going to fire, he wasn't going to steal Meera's glory or her payback. Meera knew this only too well. She moved her head closer to the weapon, taking aim.

Maj. Rana had just led a major CI/CT op that had eliminated nine hardcore terrorists without losing a beat, but this was the moment he had been waiting, hoping and praying for, for years. He aimed his gun in the direction of the three terrorists, ready to take out the other two in two clean shots as soon as Meera took down Khayyam. His heart pounded in anticipation.

The next second, Meera squeezed the trigger. The first bullet went straight through the back of the skull of the terrorist who had broken her leg just moments ago. She reloaded the gun; and in the next clean shot, she put a bullet into the head of the second terrorist who had shackled her hands. Both terrorists flanking Khayyam fell to the ground like puppets whose strings had been severed. And before a bewildered Maj. Rana could even turn towards her to gauge what was happening, why she wasn't going for Khayyam, she took the third shot. The bullet whistled through the forest and lodged itself in Khayyam's right knee and he immediately fell to the ground.

Maj. Rana turned to Meera. Her shots had been so accurate, he realized the bullet in the knee had been intentional. But he couldn't understand why. 'Meera—' he started.

She shook her head and looked him in the eye. 'Your shot, sir,' said Meera, in a low, calm voice.

What transpired between Maj. Rana and Meera in that moment was so much bigger than mere revenge. He understood her intention in a split second and felt a strange emotion in his stomach, but there was no time to waste. Maj. Rana aimed his M4A1 and shot Khayyam in the head.

He collapsed to the ground with a thud.

The rest of the commandoes were beside Meera and Maj. Rana by now, and he ordered them to confirm the kills. The commandoes followed his orders and ran to the corpses of the three dead terrorists.

Out of breath and buzzing with adrenalin at what had just happened, Maj. Rana dropped to his knees beside Meera. He looked her in the eye and then shook his head in amazement.

'Why?' he asked.

Meera shrugged; she had no regrets; she knew she had done the right thing. Despite the tears in her eyes and pain, which made her wince, there was a calmness in her voice, 'I hope the entire paltan is able to sleep well from tonight onwards, Maj. Rana, knowing that one of their own has gotten them payback.'

Maj. Rana was at a loss for words. He shook his head a few more times, his eyes filling with tears as well—a rare sight for this tough commando.

The squad radioed HQ, and handed the device to Maj. Rana, who confirmed the success of the mission to the CO, 2IC and the ministry. He also conveyed that, without any casualty on the Indian side, except for Meera's injury, the squad had confirmed kills of eleven Cat-A and A++ terrorists, including that of the infamous Khayyam Anwar. The teams at the other end of the radio broke out in loud cheers at this information.

This was a big day for the Para SF unit. Justice had been served, Ranvijay's blood had been avenged and the unit had once again lived up to its formidable image by successfully executing this high-level CI/CT operation.

They were told that air evacuation was on its way for Meera, and post-operation protocol had been set in motion. A separate party was to arrive by air in fifteen minutes to secure the area and to retrieve the bodies of the terrorists who had been eliminated by this squad.

The mission had been successful.

The evacuation chopper for Meera took twelve minutes to arrive and until then, Havaldar Siddhu and Maj. Rana sat with her. They said nothing to each other—there were no words.

When Meera, secured on a stretcher, was being taken to the helicopter, Maj. Rana spoke to her, 'You set me free today, Meera.' His voice was overcome with emotion. 'You gave me your chance . . . I can't even . . .' He was beginning to tear up.

'It was always yours, sir,' Meera interrupted him. 'Khayyam was always going to be your kill. I am glad to have assisted you.'

Maj. Rana nodded. There were no words to convey how much he appreciated what she had done today in those tense, high-pressure moments. He was astonished and so impressed by her quick reaction, even quicker thinking and her compassion.

To Maj. Rana, Ranvijay had been a hero because he was driven by his concern for the safety of a fellow commando, something Ranvijay valued more than his own life. But he believed that Meera was a hero because she put someone else's needs before her own. She put the country's safety before a peaceful life for herself. She put Maj. Rana's salvation before her own revenge. These were qualities that made her a hero.

Maj. Rana was sure that the country would talk of her bravery for years to come. For now, he hoped, she was getting all the medical help she needed and would recover soon because, while she had laid one Khayyam to rest, there were many more—and the country needed heroes like Meera.

* * *

In the Research and Referral (RR) Hospital in Delhi, where she was transferred the day after the operation, Meera thought about how differently her life had turned out from what she had imagined and planned for. She wasn't complaining, though. She knew that she wasn't just a Veer Nari or a soldier—she was so much more.

She was Meera, Ranvijay's warrior-princess, her mother and mother-in-law's hope; and in this yuddh, she had proved that she was more than worth it.

Meera had often thought about the concept of heroism, and now it came to her—maybe heroism meant putting someone else's peace of mind before yours. She was content with that.

Epilogue

It was 5 a.m., and a dense fog covered Delhi as usual. Meera had just come out of the shower and was about to get ready for the big occasion. She opened her black, metal trunk, the one that still bore Ranvijay's name painted on it in white, to take out her uniform. It was on top of the rest of her belongings, neatly ironed, folded and ready to wear. As she lifted it out, her eyes fell on another item of clothing in the trunk—the white, linen saree she had worn to the Republic Day parade in 2015, to receive the Kirti Chakra that was awarded posthumously to Ranvijay. That day, she had been lost and broken.

In five years, she was here again. But this time, she was going to be dressed in her Indian Army uniform, as the Indian Army's first woman officer to receive a Shaurya Chakra for displaying tactical acumen in army intelligence, and showcasing indomitable courage in combat, along with Maj. Rana, Havaldar Siddhu and Naik Shaktiveil, another commando from Ranvijay's Para SF unit. They were being recognized for their undeterred bravery during Op Payback.

Lightly touching the white saree, she thought about how far she had come. She wondered what Ranvijay would think of all of this . . . she missed him every day, and more on days like this. She remembered his smile and her heart skipped a beat at the warm memory. Just then, Ma knocked on her door. Meera's parents were going to accompany her to the ceremony. Her dad, overwhelmed with pride, had been unable to hold back his tears, and Ma's smile had been a mile wide since the day she told them about this award.

'Ready?' Ma asked.

'Ten minutes!' Meera called out.

In ten minutes, she stood outside her room in her crisp uniform. Her mother was waiting for her, all dressed in a new poshak. She gazed at her wordlessly.

'What?' Meera asked.

'Nothing,' Ma shrugged. 'Just—you know you're my hero, right?'

'And mine too,' her father added, appearing behind Ma.

Meera felt a surge of emotions, and she smiled at the two of them.

Heroism. Maybe it's uncomplicated. Maybe it lies in little acts of inspiring others, and in the simple ways you make your parents proud.

Together, they walked out to the army Gypsy, waiting to take them to the parade ground.

***

Meera was ushered to the end of the red carpet and within seconds, she stood on the mark which had been shown to her earlier. As she stood there at attention, the announcement began: 'Lt Meera Chauhan. Corps of Signals,' the voice announced. Meera stood still, eyes straight ahead.

'Lt Meera Chauhan was deployed in a counterinsurgency, counterterrorism operation in Kashmir in December of . . .'

Meera's mind went blank at this point, yet again. It was like déjà vu, but different. She stood there, her head held high, looking straight ahead as the voice on the microphone droned on, recounting her role in Operation Payback.

'. . . for displaying sterling tactical acumen in army intelligence, gallantry beyond the call of duty and nerves of steel in the face of hostile fire from the enemy; for eliminating two hardcore terrorists and injuring another one despite being seriously wounded herself, Lt Meera Chauhan is awarded the Shaurya Chakra,' when the announcement concluded, it was her cue.

Meera marched up to the President, who congratulated her sincerely on becoming the first woman officer of the Indian Army to receive the Shaurya Chakra and presented her with the medal. A tiny smile appeared on Meera's face as the cameras flashed, capturing the historical moment.

Heroism knows no boundaries; it is not confined to gender or role.

Heroism is not dramatic; it's the strength to keep one's composure in the face of danger. Everyone can be a hero by living for a cause which is bigger than personal gain and glory, and Meera thought that, while heroism would continue to elude her, she was at peace with the concept now.

* * *

Breaking News: Women in Combat Roles!

Report desk

Delhi, 26 January 2020:

The Indian government announced today that women will now be inducted in combat roles in the Indian Army. Women officers will now be inducted in and considered for roles in active combat duty, in frontline battalions and regiments. This is an important milestone in the journey towards equal opportunities in the armed forces.

[The news report above is fictional, like this story—but the author hopes that this soon becomes a reality. Jai Hind!]

Acknowledgements

This story took time, sweat and tears—and the help of some of the most inspiring, encouraging and brave people I've ever known. I wanted to tell the story of Veer Naris to the world, the story of the brave women in the forces and I also wanted to write about the heroism of seemingly regular people in general. This book is the result and I hope I did justice to it.

There's an entire village that helped me research, write, edit and complete this story, and I want to thank them all.

I thank my parents, for instilling the love of storytelling in me. I read because you did, and I write because you write. The two of you are my first experience with real-life heroes.

Thank you, Deepthi Talwar, for being by my side for a decade now and for being the coolest editor ever. I'm in awe of your sense of storytelling and structure (and your speed!).

Thank you, Gauri, for being the most creative ten-year-old—coming up with dramatic new twists for this story for the entire duration that I was writing it. While I couldn't include an alternative reality where Meera was a superhero with transformation powers in this story, I will try to write another story for you. And one day, I hope this story inspires you, and makes you proud.

A big thank you to my husband, Chandan. You have lived this story as much as I did, possibly even more. I'm grateful for your solid inputs, for your unwavering support and for your immense faith in me when I lacked faith in myself. You're my hero in crisp combats.

Thank you to everyone in the Indian Armed Forces, serving and retired, and their families. Thank you to my army-wife tribe.

And my biggest thank you to all the women in the Armed Forces for inspiring millions of young girls and women who see you and know that they can hope to scale greater heights too—that they can be heroes, too.

Jai Hind.